On Midnight Beach

About the Author

Marie-Louise Fitzpatrick is an Irish author and illustrator. She is a picture-book maker and also writes novels. Her books include *Izzy and Skunk*, *There*, *Owl, Bat, Bat, Owl* and *Hagwitch*. Her work has won many awards, including four CBI Book of the Year awards.

On Midnight Beach

Marie-Louise Fitzpatrick

FABER & FABER

First published in 2020
by Faber & Faber Limited
Bloomsbury House,
74–77 Great Russell Street,
London WC1B 3DA

Typeset in Garamond Premier by MRules
Printed by CPI Group (UK) Ltd, Croydon CR0 4YY

A CIP record for this book
is available from the British Library

ISBN 978–0–571–35559–4

FSC
www.fsc.org
MIX
Paper from responsible sources
FSC® C020471

8 10 9 7

The author received financial assistance from the Arts Council of Ireland in the form of a literature bursary

the arts council
an chomhairle ealaíon
funding
literature
artscouncil.ie

For Eunice, thank you for always believing.

And for everyone who remembers the long hot summer of 1976.

Prologue

Seth Cullen killed a dog when he was eight.

The dog was a Rottweiler called Rashers. He belonged to Butcher Hegarty and he roamed free around the streets of Carrig Cove. The butcher insisted his dog was a gentle giant and wouldn't hurt a fly, but we kids knew Rashers was mean because he curled his lip if you came too close. Then Rashers attacked Scrap, old Mrs Kehoe's Yorkie. Scrap was torn up so badly the vet over in Ross said the kindest thing would be to put the wee dog down.

That summer was tense – our mothers were scared to let us play on the street. I remember Mam telling me Rashers had tasted blood now and he'd want to taste it again. She told me to get away from the dog if ever I met him.

'Don't look him in the eyes, Emer,' she said. 'Walk away, don't run.'

But the day Rashers attacked, I ran. We all did.

Me and Fee and some other girls were skipping – 'Banana splits, banana splits, banana splits, and you do it like this'. The Rottie came charging around the corner onto High Street, barrelling for the flying ankles of the skipping girl, Mary Ryan. She screeched as his teeth sank into her calf. I dropped the rope and I ran. We all ran.

Except Mary. Rashers had her pinned.

I scrambled after the others to the turn in the road. The other girls kept on running. I stopped, dared to look back. Rashers still had hold of Mary. He was swinging his massive chops from side to side and she was flailing on the ground, helpless as an old shoe.

I remember wanting to go to her but I couldn't, couldn't move, not an inch. I clutched onto the wall of that corner house like it might fly away on me. I watched Rashers do his worst, while Mary's screams split the street and the girls behind me covered their eyes with their hands and the crooks of their elbows and begged me to tell them what was happening.

Seth Cullen came out of nowhere, a blond blur. He gave Rashers a quick thwack with his hurley stick as he ran behind him. Rashers dropped Mary with an outraged snarl and span in a circle to examine his backside. His huge head swung back to Mary and swung away again to look after the small figure racing up High Street.

The boy stopped, turned, waited.

The dog made his decision. He ran towards Seth, his big paws pounded the tarmac, his growl seemed to come up through the ground, come up through my bones. *Rashers will kill that boy for sure,* I was thinking as I left the safety of the wall and crept over to Mary.

The dog was nearly on Seth now. The boy stood there, his hurley stick in his right hand, staring Rashers right in the eyes, exactly like my mother had said not to.

'Run,' I whispered. 'RUN,' I yelled.

Seth didn't run. I saw the slow raise of the stick in his right hand, the toss of the ball from his left, but when he struck, it was so fast my eye couldn't follow the ball. I saw Rashers stop, as if he'd hit an invisible wall. His head flipped back, his legs buckled. He hit the ground like a sack of potatoes.

I looked at Seth, both his hands wrapped round the neck of the hurley, his arms and body coming back from the swing. I understood. He'd used the little ball as a missile. He'd fired it straight into the dog's open jaws.

For a moment nobody moved, then everyone came at once. The girls I'd been skipping with inched out onto the road. The boys came racing across from the green. They all formed a circle around the dog and the boy with the hurley stick.

Mary's leg was covered in blood. She whimpered in protest as I hauled her to her feet but I was determined to see what was happening. I put my arm around her and took her weight as we hobbled over to where Rashers had fallen. We pushed our way into the circle.

'He's dead,' someone said.

'He's pretending,' someone else said. 'He'll jump up in a minute and savage the lot of us.'

But there was no doubt. Rashers was dead. Up till then, in my imagination, death looked like sleep; that day I understood that death has its own particular stillness. Rashers' eyes were glazed, his teeth were frozen in a surprised snarl, there was blood in the white spittle foaming about his mouth, his paws were limp and heavy on the ground. He was dead, dead, dead – as dead as the half cows hanging in Butcher Hegarty's shop window, as dead as the pig's head with the wizened apple on the cracked china plate, as dead as the sheep's hearts on the metal tray, as the tripe and the rashers arranged in squelchy rows beside the heaps of dead pink sausages.

'You killed him,' Gus McRoy said. His eyes were big as balloons. 'You feckin' killed him.'

'Stone dead,' Kit Crosby said.

I stared at Seth. He was breathing hard and his hands still gripped the hurley stick, but his face at that moment was like no kid's I'd ever seen. It was contorted into a grimace and Seth Cullen was lost somewhere inside it. His skin was drawn back so tight I could see his skull. His eyes were bulging and black. His lips, normally full and soft and pink against his pale skin, were thin and bloodless, stripped back from his teeth, brand new incisors too big, too sharp in his little-boy mouth.

'Holy cow,' Gus said, slapping his friend on the back. 'What a shot! It must have been a hundred miles an hour.'

'Shame to waste a good sliotar,' Kit Crosby said. 'I'll get it for you, Seth.'

Kit knelt in front of Rashers' gaping jaws and reached a shaking hand towards those bloody fangs. There were gasps around me as everyone realised what Kit was about to do. Louise O'Toole squealed, Mary dug her fingers into my arm, but we stepped closer.

Kit counted to three under his breath and pushed his hand between Rashers' teeth. Mary wailed. The boys began to chant.

'Out, out, get it out.'

A wildness ripped through us. It spread across

Kit's face, caught every boy and most of the girls too. Gus McRoy grinned, kicked the dead dog and whooped. Conor McNessa grabbed hold of Rashers' tail and made it wag. The boys howled with laughter, the girls clutched their faces and each other.

'Out, out, get it out.'

Kit began clowning with his hand inside the dog's mouth. He let on he'd sunk his arm halfway down the dog's throat and he couldn't find the ball.

'Out, out, get it out.'

He pretended Rashers had him.

'LEMME GO, LEMME GO, LEMME GO!' he yelled, thrashing around, eyes popping, fighting off Rashers with his free arm. We were all yelling, screaming, squirming. When he pulled his hand back out and held the little leather ball above his head, we cheered. He wiped it clean on the leg of his shorts and presented it to Seth, whose eyes were returning to their usual colours – one green, one blue.

I saw. I saw the rage slide off his skin like a passing shadow.

He tossed the killing ball up into the sky. We raised our faces to watch it fly above us, higher, higher, till it stalled at last and fell back, back to Seth's outstretched hand. We cheered again.

Grown-ups arrived, running, frowning, calling

out. Mary's mother, mine, Fee's, Seth's. And Butcher Hegarty. He let out a roar when he saw his dog lying there. When he saw the blood-red ball, the hurley in Seth's hand, the exultant look on Seth's face, I thought he was going to belt him. But Mary's mother began yelling, 'Look at Mary's leg. Look what that horrible brute of yours has done to my Mary's leg. She'll need stitches, there'll be scars.'

Mr Hegarty looked at Mary's leg. He looked at all of us. He looked down at his dog. He shut his mouth and said nothing. He crouched beside Rashers. We looked at the ground as he stroked his dog's head a few times, then he quickly swiped his sleeve across his face and hoisted Rashers onto his shoulder like a side of beef. He stood up and walked away.

Mary was bawling now, sitting on the ground again with her leg stuck out in front of her. There were sharp intakes of breath as Seth's mother gently peeled the lacy sock away from her calf. Blood trickled from multiple puncture marks and one area was a mangled mess of exposed flesh. I felt terrible for making Mary walk.

'Seth saved Mary, Mrs Ryan,' I said. 'I think Rashers would have killed her if Seth hadn't drawn him off.'

'He killed that dog with one blow, Mrs Ryan,'

Gus McRoy said, and he mimicked Seth swinging the hurley stick. Gus was the leader of the Carrig Cove boys; whatever he did, they all did. They all began tossing imaginary balls into the air and thwacking them with imaginary hurleys, slamming them down imaginary dog gullets.

The mothers turned away and began tending to Mary's leg. Deirdre Cullen offered to make a herbal paste for the wounds and Mary's mother, who normally wouldn't give Seth's mam the time of day, mustered a stiff smile as she refused and said she'd be taking Mary to the hospital. The other mothers gathered us girls and brought us home to play house with our plastic tea sets and Crolly dollies, safe in the backyards where they could watch us. The boys were left outside to hunt imaginary enemies, their hurley-shaped guns loaded with imaginary leather bullets.

After the killing of Rashers, Seth Cullen was god to the other boys in Carrig Cove. Gus McRoy took to calling him Dog and within days everyone was doing it. No one ever called him Seth again, not even the adults, not even his own mam. He became Dog Cullen, in honour of the day he killed Butcher Hegarty's Rottweiler.

I've never forgotten that day – the fear that

tore through us when Rashers attacked, the strange wildness which took hold when we knew the dog was dead. I've never forgotten the way us kids turned from scared rabbits to victorious wolf pack, or Seth Cullen's face as he stood over the corpse of the butcher's dog. Seth had saved my friend Mary but he'd been blooded like Rashers had been when he mangled Mrs Kehoe's Yorkie. It frightened me and I stayed clear of him after that.

Don't look him in the eyes, Emer. Walk away. Run.

I kept clear of Dog Cullen. Till the summer we turned seventeen, the summer the dolphin came to Ross Bay. That summer I looked in Dog Cullen's eyes – one green, one blue – and I forgot to walk away.

I

1
Emer

I wasn't on the beach the day the dolphin came. It was my friend Fedelma and her kid brother Rory that spotted him and they came running to the shop like mad things, bursting to tell me.

'There's a dolphin in the bay, Emer,' Fee said. 'You've got to come.' I was stacking cans of baked beans on the second shelf, centre aisle.

'She doesn't "got to" anything,' Da said, looking up from his ledgers. 'What's so urgent about a dolphin in the bay? You'd think you'd never seen one before.'

'Not like this, Mr Monaghan. This one's in really close, Mr Monaghan,' Fee said, sauntering over to the sweet counter and leaning her chin on the top of the glass. 'It's a once in a lifetime opportunity, Mr Monaghan. You wouldn't want to deprive Emer of that?'

Da rolled his eyes. 'You needn't be trying that "I'm-a-proper-caution" act on me, Fedelma Hennessy,' he said. 'This is a family business and it takes a family to run it. No one here has time to be gallivanting after dolphins.'

'What's this?' Mam said, coming through to the shop from the house. 'There are dolphins in the bay?'

'Just the one, Mrs Monaghan,' Fee said. 'It's practically on the beach, it's so close. Me and Rory thought Emer'd want to see it.'

'Emer has work to do,' Da said.

'Do you have the shelves stacked, Emer?' Mam said.

I nodded.

'Well then, it's almost closing time, Syl. She's been working every day since the summer holidays began. Let her go.'

Da scowled and turned back to his ledgers. That was answer enough for me.

'It'll be gone by the time ye get to the beach, or fetched up on the stones breathing its last,' I heard him saying, but I was already shrugging off my shop coat. I was out the door before he could change his mind.

'Is there really a dolphin or is this one of your mad plans to get me out of the shop?' I asked, as we raced down Main Street.

'There is a dolphin, Emer. There is,' Rory said between breaths.

'We thought it was a feckin' shark,' Fee said, grabbing Rory's hand and pulling him behind her. 'I swear to God, when we saw the fin cutting through the water so close to shore the pair of us screeched like feckin' herring gulls. Then it stuck its face up over the waves and we saw that daft smile. I nearly pissed myself laughing.'

Fee and me had made the mistake of taking Rory to see *Jaws* in February and he'd had a real horror of the sea ever since. When school broke, Fee began dragging him to the beach every day to see if she could walk the fear out of him. Now here he was racing with us down to the shore. I glanced back over my shoulder to smile at him.

'Watch out!' a voice said.

I turned to see two startled faces, right in my path. I tried to stop, lost my balance, began to spin out onto the road. Hands closed around my wrists and jerked me back on to the footpath. I found myself looking into a pair of laughing eyes – one green, one blue.

'Sorry, sorry, I'm . . . sorry,' I said.

'No problem,' Dog Cullen said. He let go my wrists and stepped away from me. His friend, Kit Crosby, was behind him. 'Where's the fire?' he said.

'No fire,' said Rory. 'There's a dolphin. On the beach.'

'On the beach? You mean it's dead?' Kit said.

'No,' Fee said. 'He means it's close to shore and we're going to look at it.'

'Cool,' Kit said. 'Mind if we tag along?'

I tried to catch Fee's eye but she said, 'No law against it, I suppose,' and cocked an eyebrow at Kit before she turned to walk on. Rory ran ahead, suddenly brave. I fell in behind Fee and Kit.

'Hi,' Dog said.

'Hi,' I said.

We crunched across the stones to the water's edge and stood in a ragged line, scanning the water. The sea was choppy, full of shifting grey triangles. There were a dozen false alarms before we spotted it.

'There!' said Fee, pointing. 'There it is.'

'There?'

'There!'

'There.'

A fin flashed dark against the incoming white foam and we caught glimpses of face and tail as it came closer in. Without saying anything we all kicked off our runners and rolled up the legs of our jeans – Rory too. The dolphin stuck its head above the waves, appearing to watch us wade out towards it.

We stopped in a row, the water slapping against our thighs, our jeans getting soaked.

The dolphin disappeared, resurfaced, down, up, down, as if it was drawing a parallel line in the sea and marking each of us along it, acknowledging us – one, two, three, four, five. Fee bobbed it a watery curtsy and we laughed and bobbed too. We touched one another's arms and said, 'Look!' and 'Do you see it?' and 'Oh!' as if Dog and Kit were friends of Rory, Fee and me, not familiar strangers.

The dolphin chuckled at us and flicked us a knowing side-eye as it swam quickly back along its parallel line, pushing a wave of water towards the beach. I would have lost my footing if Dog hadn't caught my hand. The dolphin turned again and sent another wave our way, and Dog still held my hand and I held his and I held Rory's and Rory was holding Fee's and she was holding Kit Crosby's and all of us were shrieking.

Then the fin disappeared and the sea calmed down and we stood there, staring out. Staring. Staring. Just long enough to realise we were holding hands. I blushed. I'd held Rory's hand a hundred times, swinging him down the road, Fee on his other side, running to catch the school bus. My left hand holding Rory's was fine and dandy. My right hand caught inside Dog Cullen's fingers – it was on fire. My heart was thumping, my eyes never left the water, but my left hand and my brain were panicking. *Do I let go? Do I wait for him to? Does he think I'm an idiot for holding on so long? Will he think I'm strange if I pull away?*

'There!' yelled Fee, pointing. 'There.'

The fin had appeared way out in the bay and was heading towards us at speed, coming at us, coming in. Somehow I knew Kit had Fee's hand and we were all attached again. Just when it looked as if the dolphin would leave it too late to turn, it swerved. Its tail sent a wave towards us, so hard and fast that we hadn't time to react. We went down like skittles.

We came up, gasping and spluttering salt water, struggling to our feet, going down again as another wave hit. I flailed about trying to get back on my feet but I was laughing hard and blinded by seawater. Two hands came from behind me, caught me under my arms, pulled me upright and held me.

That's three times, I thought. *Three times inside an hour I've fallen and Dog Cullen has caught me.*

'Are you all right?' Dog said, his face against my hair, his lips close to my ear.

'Ye-ah, yeah, I'm grand,' I said. He smiled at me. I don't know if I smiled back. I know my cheeks were burning. I think I may have turned away. I think I may have said something stupid to Fee, something moronic like, 'Are you wet?'

'What do you think?' she said. 'I'm feckin' soaked through to my knickers, is what I am.'

Kit cracked up as if Fee had made the funniest joke ever. We all laughed. We fell about, knocking against each other and making a show of fighting to stay upright as the waves tugged at our soaked clothes, trying to pull us back in. I saw Fee clutch at Kit and giggle, and he grabbed her, then stood back and did a mock wobble, windmilling his arms around before tumbling backwards. Rory stumbled and reached for Dog, and Dog caught and set him upright, the same way he'd done me. I laughed.

My teeth began to chatter. I set them into a smile, brushed my hair out of my face and twisted it in my hands, though it wasn't really wet. I considered faking a stumble so Dog could touch me again. *I want him to touch me again,* I thought. But I couldn't do it, couldn't be so coy.

An hour ago I was stacking cans of beans in the shop, I thought, *and now I'm on the beach, soaked to the skin and wondering how to flirt with the prettiest boy in Carrig Cove.*

We waited in the water another few minutes till we were sure the dolphin had gone for good, then we waded back to shore. Dog and me walked up the beach behind the others. I didn't know what to do with my hands so I crossed them in front of me and hugged my body as if I was freezing, which I was. I let my teeth do their worst. I tried to look at Dog without him seeing me do it. His blond hair was dripping onto his shoulders and his grey sweatshirt was stuck to him.

'D'you think it'll come back?' he said, looking straight at me.

'Maybe,' I said.

'Kit and me will come again tomorrow to see if it does. Will you and Fedelma be here?' he said.

'Maybe,' I said. 'If Da'll let me off the shop.'

'I hope he does,' he said, and he nodded at Rory and Fee as he and Kit walked away over the stones towards the gap in the wall that led out to Main Street.

2
Emer

The next day, proper summer arrived in Carrig Cove. True blue summer, twenty degrees and rising. It would be the hottest summer we'd ever know in Donegal but that day we thought the good weather was a one-off, a pet day to make the most of. Mam convinced Da to let me out of work at lunchtime and I stuffed my togs and a towel into a bag and ran down to the beach. Fee and Rory were already there and Dog and Kit were with them. I felt my cheeks grow hot.

Stop being ridiculous, I told myself. *They're just a couple of boys you've known forever. Are you going to turn beetroot every time you meet them?*

I ducked my head down so my hair fell across my cheeks and I slowed to a walk.

'Right, let's go,' Fee said as I came near. She

jumped to her feet, shedding clothes till she was down to her apple-green swimsuit. Dog and Kit stripped to their trunks. They looked at me.

'Did you not change at home?' Fee asked. She rolled her eyes. 'Come on, let's leave her to it or she'll die of embarrassment.'

Typical Fee. Typical Fee to know I'd be mortified if I had to struggle into my swimsuit in front of boys and typical Fee to decide the best way to save me the mortification was by drawing attention to it.

She waltzed off down the beach, her red hair swinging, and Kit followed her. Dog gave me a quick smile and went too.

'I'll wait for you, Emer,' Rory said.

'Go on after them, I'm all right,' I said.

It came out sharper than I intended and Rory's face fell. He stood up slowly and trailed after Dog. I began the towel dance, clutching at the corners of my ancient beach towel and fumbling with zips and straps until my jeans and T-shirt were a heap at my feet and I was in my swimsuit. To my horror it seemed to have shrunk since last year. I tugged at it, yanking it down around my thighs and up at my shoulders, trying to get as much of me inside it as possible but as I walked across the sand I felt it shrink.

Fee and Kit were in the water, Rory and Dog were

waiting for me, Dog watching me approach. I found I couldn't walk normally. Placing one foot in front of the other became a strange slow-motion awkwardness of out-of-sync feet, knees, hips. I broke into a run.

'Come on, Rory,' I shouted, pulling his arm as I went by. 'Last one in is a rotten egg.'

Rory jerked his arm free and I left him behind and plunged on into the water. Straight in. I didn't care how icy it was as long as I was inside it, my body hidden. I didn't turn my head but I knew Dog was right behind me. As soon as I surfaced I saw the fin coming towards us in the distance.

'D'you see it?' Fee shouted, somewhere over to my left. I nodded. The fin came closer then turned, came again and turned, like an invitation: *Come on, come on, come closer.*

I badly wanted to look around and see how near Dog was. I could have let on like I was checking for Rory but I'd probably have fooled no one, so I didn't let myself do it. Instead I kept my eyes straight ahead and began swimming out towards the dolphin, like I was in a race and meant to win it.

I was so distracted I forgot to remember that dolphins swim faster than humans. Suddenly the dolphin surfaced in front of me, exhaling from its blowhole with a loud whoosh. I had to stop myself mid-stroke. It was arm's length away, its eye looking at mine. I heard myself gasp and almost choked on a mouthful of salt water. I half-turned my head to check where the others were. Miles away, is where. Halfway back to the beach, three heads in the water, eyes staring. I'd swum too far, too fast, and now I was on my own with a wild animal that could kill me with a twist of its tail.

My heart was beating like the hammers of hell, my ears were thrumming. I knew I should swim away but I was frozen in place. I kept my eye on the animal and it kept its eye on me. It circled around me and I turned with it. I took a deep breath and pushed my terror down.

You'll never be this close to a wild thing again, Emer, I told myself. *Don't waste time being scared.*

The dolphin moved slowly, as if it understood that it could hurt me. Up close it didn't look like Flipper off of the telly or the shiny pretty dolphins on the greeting cards in our shop. It was covered in scrapes and gouges – random slashes near face and fin and tail, parallel lines hatched its sides as if someone had raked its skin with a pitchfork, a nick out of its dorsal fin the size of a fifty-pence piece. There was one particularly vicious mark along its right side and a single white scar that ran above and below its left eye, like the marks clowns paint on. The eye between the marks was watching me.

Its eye looked mischievous, its mouth was open in an absurd grin. It came closer. I could have touched it, could have stroked its head. I told myself that wasn't a real smile, that it was just the way a dolphin's mouth naturally turned (*would you look at all those needle-like teeth*), but still some kind of joy welled up inside me and I found myself grinning back at it. It made a noise that sounded like a chuckle and I answered with a single delighted 'Ha'.

Everything stopped, everything was still. We floated in front of each other, sizing one another up. There was nothing in this world but me and this creature. Without thinking I stretched my arm towards it, fingers slowly reaching towards its face. It made a buzzing, clicking sound and I caught myself, hesitated. Its eye drifted from me, distracted by some movement to my right.

Fee. She was a few feet behind me treading water, her eyes wide. The dolphin went to her, circled her, checking her out as it had me. Fee laughed softly and the dolphin flipped its nose and whistled a greeting. Fee reached her hand out like I had and the dolphin ducked away from her. But it came back. And then Fee and me were laughing out loud and the dolphin was swimming around the both of us and would have stayed, I think, if Dog and Kit hadn't swum closer. The dolphin ducked beneath the surface. Fee and me went under after it, eyes open, but it was swimming away, swimming towards Dog and Kit.

It passed them, close and quick, so close they had to avoid it. They'd just gathered themselves when it came back at them, aimed straight at them, but veered away in time. A third swim-by and it was gone, off into the heart of the bay, back out to sea.

'So I'm guessing it's a bull,' Kit said when we were back on the beach, wrapped up in towels. 'Flirts with the girls and plays tough with the boys.'

'Yez are just chickens,' Fee said, flopping down in a heap on the warm sand.

'Rory is the chicken,' Kit said. 'He never came in at all, stayed in the shallows like a lickle-ickle yellow baby. Puck puck puck.' He jumped to his feet and flapped his arms up and down. He began a silly Monty Python-esque walk, knees locked together, feet stuck out like a duck. 'Puck puck puck,' he said. 'Puck puck puck.'

Rory's chin tucked to his chest and he frowned at the sand, trying not to cry in front of the older boys. He'd have been anxious as hell watching us lot out in the water. The fact that he'd ventured into the sea at all, had stood in the shallows waiting, was a minor victory for him. He'd been brave, braver than any of us given his fear of the water. A glance at Fee told me she was ready to clobber Kit.

'So, what are we going to call it . . . him?' asked Dog, casually reaching out an arm as Kit goose-stepped past us again. He snagged Kit's ankle, toppling him over on the sand. 'Oops,' Dog said, and we all laughed.

'Oops would be a pretty terrible name for a dolphin,' I said and winked at Rory, trying to knock a smile out of him. Dog grinned at me and Fee relaxed enough to say, 'Flipper.'

'Too obvious,' Kit said, rolling upright, covered head to toe in coarse Carrig Cove sand. 'Skippy,' he said. 'Skippeeeee, Skippeeee, Skippeeee the Ross Bay Dol-o-phin,' he sang.

'You're a right plank,' Fee said, looking away.

'Shadow,' I said. 'Shade for short.'

'Yes, but in Irish,' Dog said. *'Scáthach.'*

'Too poetic,' Fee said. 'We need something short and catchy.' She clicked her fingers in the air to demonstrate.

'Scar, then,' I said. 'He has loads of them on his body and one across his left eye.'

'That doesn't sound friendly,' Fee said. 'It has to be friendly because he's a friendly dolphin.'

'Are you sure of that?' Kit said. 'Maybe he's just messin' with our heads, reeling us in, waiting till we feel safe, and then . . .' He lay flat on his stomach, stuck one elbow up behind him in imitation of a fin and began to slide forward on the sand. 'Dun dun. Dun dun. Dun dun. Dun dun dun dun dun dun . . .'

'Will you give over?' Fee snapped, but Rory was already on his feet walking up the beach, arms pinned stiffly by his sides. 'Oh, for God's sake,' Fee said. I wasn't sure whether her annoyance was aimed at Kit or Rory, or maybe she'd enough for the both of them.

She stood up and jerked her jeans on over her damp togs. 'Emer, Dog,' she said, ignoring Kit. She grabbed the rest of her stuff and ran after her brother.

Kit's face was comical. You'd think he was five and someone had burst his birthday balloon.

'Nice going, Don Juan,' Dog said, nudging Kit with his foot. 'It's OK to be nice if you like her, you know. We won't think any less of you, will we, Emer?'

I smiled and Kit made a noise that sounded like 'hum-umph,' but could have been 'Eff off.' He got to his feet. 'I'm going back in the water,' he muttered. 'Wash this sand off.'

I began to dry myself, suddenly self-conscious now I was alone with Dog. That was when I realised the towel I was wrapped in wasn't mine. It was two shades of blue, mine was candy stripes. It was Dog's towel I'd had around me ever since we came out of the water.

'Oh,' I said, pulling it away from my body and holding it out to him. 'I grabbed it by mistake.'

'No bother,' he said. There was a glint in his eye as he took it from me but his cheeks turned a little pink as he wrapped it around himself. My cheeks were flaming. I picked up my towel and looked away as he began to rub his skin. Neither of us said anything for a few minutes. When we had our clothes on he said, 'Kit's a grand fella but he doesn't always know when to stop.'

'I can see that,' I said.

'He likes your friend,' he said.

'He won't get very far with her if he keeps picking on Rory,' I said.

'No,' Dog said. 'I think even Kit may have worked that one out.' He hadn't put his T-shirt on yet and he hung his towel, wet from me, around his pale shoulders like a cape.

'Same time tomorrow?' he asked. 'If your da lets you out of the shop?' He smiled at me and double dimples flickered in his cheeks. He went from fairly good-looking to gorgeous in a split second. I stared, the words I was about to say knocked clean out of my head.

Get a grip, Emer Monaghan, I thought, *before you turn into a mindless twit like Louise O'Toole. He's only being nice. He probably doesn't mean anything by it.*

I blinked and smiled. 'If Fee isn't still mad at Kit,' I said.

'Maybe you could put in a good word for him?' Dog said. 'Tell her how tragic he looked when she left?'

'Maybe,' I said.

'Tomorrow then,' he said.

'Tomorrow,' I said and I headed up the beach.

Kit likes Fee, put in a good word for him, Dog had said. *Maybe this hanging out together on the beach is all for Kit's benefit,* I told myself.

But a part of me knew it wasn't, knew Dog liked me, knew he was watching me walk away. And I knew I liked him. Liked his face and his eyes. Liked his smile. Knew I needed to come back to the beach the next day. Knew there wasn't a hope in hell Da would give me another day off but I'd have to find a way to make him.

3
Emer

It was Mam who swung me the day off. She said she'd help Da in the shop.

'What about your bad back?' Da said, no sympathy in his voice, only a familiar whine of resentment. My mother had pulled her back lifting boxes a few years before and it had never come right. Dr Scanlon had ordered her to stay out of the shop and that hadn't gone down well with my da.

Mam said, 'As long as I don't go hefting anything, I'll be fine.' And just like that I was free.

Fee's face when she opened her front door was priceless.

'Your da's going soft,' she said. 'Maybe he's going to turn sweet and cuddly in his dotage. I'd have put money on him turning into a world-class crotchety shite.'

'Mam went to work on him,' I said. 'Where's Rory? Is he not coming?'

'I've been trying to talk him round all morning,' Fee said. 'He's afraid that prize eejit Kit Crosby's going to make fun of him again.'

'I don't think he will,' I said. 'You should have seen his face when you left. He was like a lost puppy dog.'

'Huh,' she said. She turned to yell up the stairs, 'Ror! Emer's here. She's coming to the beach with us. Come on down.'

A noise at the top of the stairs and Rory's carrot-top appeared at the bannisters.

'Come on, Rory,' I said. 'If the dolphin comes we'll need you to stand watch for us, like yesterday.'

He came down step by step, dragging one arm behind him along the rail. 'You don't want me there,' he said.

'Of course we do,' I said. 'Please, Ror. I've been given a whole day off from the shop and I know who I want to spend it with – you and Fee.'

'And those boys,' Rory said.

'If they turn up,' I said. 'If they don't it'll just be us three, and that's fine too.'

'Jesus, we're saints,' Fee whispered as he ran back up to get his towel. 'I suppose one of these years he'll toughen up. Until then we're all he's got.'

I nodded. Rory was the kid that other kids like to torment. He'd turned thirteen but looked eleven. Small, skinny, pale, he had gigantic milk-bottle glasses that took up most of his face. He looked like the Milky Bar Kid, if the Milky Bar Kid had red hair and no chocolate bars. In school they went at him for being a brainbox and teacher's pet. On the football pitch the boys called him a sissy and stuck him between the goalposts, then blamed him for every ball that got past him.

He'd had a miserable first year in Ballyfin secondary school. His classmates had tied him to lampposts, locked him in sheds, tossed his runners up onto the overhead wires, nicked his schoolbag. If Fee and me didn't drag Rory around with us, he'd have had to stay home. I didn't really mind, but sometimes it'd have been nice not to have him always around. Today was one of those sometimes, but I wanted to make up for snapping at him yesterday.

'Rory, come on, we're going,' Fee yelled, and we walked out the door.

It was warm, even though it was only nine o'clock.

'We'll be wearing shorts at this rate,' Fee said.

'I haven't got any,' I said. 'I was ten last time Mam bought me a pair.'

'Dig out an old pair of jeans,' Fee said. 'Come around to mine tonight and we'll cut them up really short. We can fray the edges like they do in *Jackie*. I have some groovy patches we can sew on the pockets. We'll be so cool.'

I tried to picture us walking around the streets of Carrig Cove got up like the girls in the *Jackie* magazine, all shiny hair and blue eye shadow, in short shorts and tight knit tops with our belly buttons showing. I started to laugh.

'Da'll have kittens,' I said, 'and your mam'll fetch Father Allan to have us exorcised.'

'OK, so maybe not as short as the girls in *Jackie*, then,' Fee said. 'But short enough to show off our super-sexy snow white legs.'

Rory caught up with us as we got to the beach. He shrank back behind us when he saw Kit and Dog already there, sitting by the rocks. There were other kids scattered around the strand. I nodded over to Louise O'Toole and Mary Ryan.

'Hi,' Dog and Kit said to me and Fee. Then, 'Hi Rory, how's it going?' Dog said.

'Yeah, hi, Rory,' said Kit. 'How's it going?'

'F-fine,' Rory said, not quite coming out from behind Fee. He looked down and began fumbling with a toggle on his rucksack. 'It's going OK, I guess,' he muttered.

We sat down.

'Are ye here for the day?' Dog asked.

'Yep,' Fee said. 'The world must be about to end. Emer's da gave her the whole day off, with a possibility of another one tomorrow. I'm surprised the sun isn't spinning in the sky.'

'Any sign of the dolphin yet?' I asked.

'Rinn?' Dog said. 'Not a ripple.'

'Rinn?' I said. 'As in the Irish for point?'

'Yeah,' Dog said. 'Rinn for his fin. Fee said it had to be short and snappy. What d'ya think?'

'I like it,' I said. 'Suits him. Cute but with an edge to it. Literally.'

'All agreed?' Dog said. 'OK then.' He stood up for a moment and held his arms out to the sea. 'Dolphin,' he shouted, 'thy name is Rinn.'

'Someone tell me when he shows,' Fee said. 'Till then I'm going to work on my freckles.' She lay back on the sand, fanned her mane of red curls out about her head and turned her face up to the sun.

'I'll go look,' Rory said. 'I'll shout when I see him.' He stood up and walked down the beach to the water.

Fee sat back up and looked at me. 'Did that just happen?' she said. 'I could barely get him down here last week, he was that scared. Now look.'

'Good for him,' Dog said.

'Yeah,' Kit said.

Fee flashed Kit a look that'd flatten a horse.

'I wasn't being sarky,' he said.

'You'd better not have been,' Fee said.

She was about to lie back down when we heard voices coming onto the beach. We turned to look. Conor McNessa and his usual gang of lads, carrying rolled towels under their arms. They strolled over and stood around us, blocking the sun.

'Hey,' Conor said to Dog.

'Hey,' Dog said.

'So, a dolphin comes into the bay and Dog Cullen goes swimming with it,' Conor said. 'Typical. You're something else, man.' Conor shook his head in admiration. He leaned down to Dog and they slapped hands in mid-air. 'I wouldn't be in a hurry to get in the water with that thing. Second cousin to sharks, they are. You've balls of steel, man.'

'And what about my balls?' Kit said, pulling a mock-offended face and flapping his hands in the general direction of his crotch. 'I was there, I swam with it too.'

'Of course you did. We all know that where Dog Cullen goes, Kit-kat Crosby follows.' Conor smiled. It was a trick of his I'd noticed before – to say something mean or sharp or plain nasty, then conjure up this charming smile that seemed to knock the harm out of it. Sure enough everyone laughed. Kit laughed along as if he didn't mind being the butt of the joke.

'Actually, it was Emer swam to it first,' Fee said, 'and none of us went as close as she did.'

'Yeah, right,' Conor said, and raised an eyebrow.

'It was too,' Dog said. 'And Fee here was right behind her. Kit and myself stayed well back. Once we were sure it wasn't going to eat them we swam in and took over.'

'Hah! Nice one, man,' Conor said.

Dog winked at Fee and myself. 'If he comes today, the girls will show you how it's done,' he said. 'Then you can try it out for yourself.'

Conor's smile slipped and a flicker of panic crossed his handsome face.

'Oh, come on, man,' Dog said. 'You'll not be having it said the girls have bigger balls than you?'

A tiny hesitation, then Conor laughed. 'Jesus,' he said. 'Walked myself into that one, didn't I?'

'Yes, you did,' Dog said. 'At full tilt.'

'And by the way,' Kit said, 'we're pretty certain the dolphin's a bull. Likes the ladies but plays rough with the lads.'

Conor groaned. 'Now he tells me,' he said, rubbing his hands across his face in exaggerated despair to amuse his audience, which had grown. Louise and Mary and the other girls had drifted over to see what was going on.

'We've named him Rinn.' Rory's voice piped up from behind Fee and everyone turned to look at him.

Conor turned his smile on Rory. 'Rinn,' he said. 'And why's that?'

'Rinn for his f-fin,' Rory said, his voice falling to a mumble under the gaze of so many eyes. 'Emer says he's covered in s-scars.'

'What did you say? What did he say?' Conor turned to us for a translation, his voice edged with impatience, shoulders and hands raised.

'The dolphin is covered in scrapes and scars,' I said.

'Scars?' Conor said.

'A heap of them,' I said. 'He has one across his left eye.'

Conor's jaw dropped slightly and he allowed me a little of the admiration he'd been showering on Dog. 'You swam that close?' he said. 'Right, lads.' He turned to his pals. 'Better get our swimming trunks on. We're going in. Can't be beat by a couple of lassies.'

'It's not here yet,' Mary Ryan said.

'He may appear if we go in,' Kit said. 'That's what happened yesterday.'

'Rory here is the best for spotting him,' Dog said. 'He's standing lookout for us today, aren't you Rory?'

Rory nodded, his glasses nearly falling off his face in his eagerness. Fee smiled her thanks to Dog: he'd managed to neatly include Rory and get him out of any actual swimming at the same time. Everyone scattered across the beach to shed their clothes.

'Can't stand that Conor McNessa guy,' Fee whispered to me as we got to our feet. 'Don't know what the other lads see in him. Dog's worth ten of him.'

I nodded. I'd never been keen on Conor McNessa, though everyone other than Fee and myself seemed to think he was the main man. Gus McRoy had been the king of the Carrig Cove boys when we were kids but his family had moved across the bay to Ross six years ago and Conor had taken over as leader of the gang. The lads walking around him in a herd, hanging on his every word. The girls – Louise O'Toole and Karen Cox in particular – drooled over him and spent every other minute discussing what it would be like to go with him.

'Ready?' Fee asked. 'Let's show those snot-nosed boys how it's done.' She jumped up and went running for the water, and me right behind her. Dog and Kit came after us and we waded in, calling, 'Rinn!

Rinn!' as if the dolphin would know we'd given him a name.

Within minutes Rory was shouting and pointing out the approaching fin. We waded towards it, our hands linked. Dog smiled at me and then we let go and swam forward together. The dolphin came, as curious as before, and we went closer to show the others on the beach how brave we were. After a while some of them came in and Rinn left us to investigate the new bodies. Fee and me swam back to shore, passing Conor, Phelim and JJ heading out.

'Safety in numbers,' Fee whispered to me. 'Never the first into the fray, our Conor.'

Rinn stayed around for hours that day. Even Louise and Mary got in to swim with him after a while, though they didn't go close. Rory read his book, Dog and Kit joined the other lads in a game of football, Fee and myself basked in the sun and headed back into the water every now and then to cool off. It was a good day, though I agreed with Rory when he said he preferred it when it was just us – him and Fee and me, Kit and Dog . . . and Rinn.

'It won't be like that again,' Fee said. 'From now on, for as long as he stays around, it'll be a beach-full of people and everyone vying to get Rinn's attention.'

I stared out at the water. 'Maybe we shouldn't have named him,' I said. 'We claimed a wild thing and lost it in the same breath.'

4

Emer

Fee rolled her eyes. 'Jaysus, you're melodramatic. Us naming Rinn had nothing to do with it. The sun is splitting the stones so there was always going to be a rush to the beach. And we can hardly expect people not to notice a dolphin lepping around in full view of the village, can we?'

Despite her words I could hear her disappointment. 'The faces on us,' she said.

We glanced at each other. Fee looked as if someone had killed her cat and I suppose I looked the same. Kit and Ror were frowning. Dog was chewing his lip.

'Rory's right,' Dog said. 'It was better with just us five.' He screwed up his eyes and a small smile began to tug at the corner of his mouth.

'What?' Kit said. 'You've got an idea, haven't you?'

'I might have,' Dog said. 'What time is it?

'Five thirty-five,' I said.

'Right,' Dog said, getting to his feet and brushing the sand off his legs. 'We're going to Paudy Bán's.'

'But what—'

'Come on.' He grinned down at us and walked away.

We scrambled to our feet, grabbed our towels and bags, and followed him off the beach.

Paudy Bán's was the pub at the end of Main Street – the pub at the end of the world, my mother called it. The road ran out at Paudy's. It widened to a large circle so people could turn their cars and drive back towards civilisation.

The pub opened at five-thirty. As we approached it we could see there was already a group of men gathered outside. Mickser McCabe, old Willie Henry, Tom and Ben Fitz were perched in the windowsills, clutching whiskeys and biting down on their clay pipes; the younger men were standing with pints in one hand and cigarettes in the other.

'Wait here,' Dog said to us when we were still a few doors shy of the pub. He walked on, making straight for Dan Fogarty. Dan owned the *Ella Louise*. Mam had told me this morning that someone in the shop told her they'd heard that the dolphin had followed the *Ella Louise* home the other morning, trailing the trawler into Ross Bay a few hours before Fee and Rory spotted him.

We watched as Dog began speaking to Dan and his mate, Jim. Dan's eyebrows rose as he listened. He rubbed his chin, said something. Dog pointed towards us lot loitering by a wall. Dan frowned. We saw him purse his lips as if he was thinking something over, then he smiled and nodded his head. Dog shook Dan's hand and waved to the rest of the men. The old men tipped their fingers to their caps in salute, the younger men jutted their chins slightly in acknowledgement. Willie Henry put his hand out to Dog to keep him a moment, to ask him a question, something hurling-related, no doubt. Willie's face creased into a delighted gap-toothed smile as he listened to Dog's answer. Then Dog came strolling back to us, his hands in his jean pockets, his long hair floating back from his face, his eyes lit up.

'We're in,' he said. 'We're to be at the pier at six-thirty sharp tomorrow morning. Dan says to bring jumpers and windcheaters because it'll get nippy out there.'

'You never?' Kit said, his face splitting into a huge grin as he turned to us. 'He's only convinced Dan Fogarty to take us out on the *Ella Lou*. Jesus! I've always wanted to go out on one of the trawlers. I spent a whole year in primary school sucking up to Phelim Roche in the hope he'd get his da to take us out.'

'All of us?' I asked Dog. 'Dan'll bring all of us?' I knew a lot of the fishermen believed letting a woman on board would bring them bad luck.

'All of us. Rory too,' Dog said, reaching out to slap Rory's arm. 'Are you pleased?' he said, and there was no denying he was directing that question at me.

I nodded and smiled. I was thinking, *It's amazing, it'll be amazing, but what if Da won't let me go? How do I convince Da to let me go?*

'It's amazing,' I said. 'It'll be amazing.'

But when Fee, Rory and me parted ways with the lads I turned to Fee.

'Da?' I said.

She put her head on one side and considered. 'Say you've been off most of the week so they may as well give you Friday as well and be done with it. Say that if this is your last day off this summer then a boat trip would put the tin hat on it.'

Rory giggled. They knew Da had said I was going back to work on Friday even if it was as hot out as 'the bloomin' Bay-hamas'.

'No way Da'll agree to me going if he knows Dog and Kit will be there,' I said.

'So don't tell him,' Fee said. 'I won't be

broadcasting who's going to my ma, that's for sure. She'd have a fit.' She looked sternly at Rory. 'I'll do the asking when we get home, right? Whatever you do, don't go mentioning Kit or Dog's names in front of Ma. D'you hear me, Ror?'

Rory nodded.

I bit my lip. I was lousy at lying but I wanted to go so I'd need to get my story straight. If I kept it vague, chances were Mam and Da would assume it was a bunch of girls going. Da would never agree if he knew we were going with lads, let alone with Dog Cullen. The men in Carrig Cove loved Dog – they thought he was a fine lad, the best. But not Da. He thought Dog was a 'right pup' – I'd heard him say so enough times. I took a deep breath as I went in the house. I was prepared to lie but in the end I didn't have to. Da went off on a tirade the moment I mentioned the dolphin.

'Is this what the world's coming to?' he growled. 'Young ones spending their summer mooning around, half-naked, chasing a piece of blubber around the bay because they think they're communing with nature or some such nonsense. Next thing we'll be having "flower power" and all that "peace, man" rubbish. I thought Dan Fogarty had more sense. Don't dolphins eat their body weight in fish a day? Does he not think about that?'

'But may I go?' I asked.

Mam nodded, Da grunted. I went into the kitchen to make a packed lunch. I stayed out of sight for the rest of the evening and headed to bed early in case Da changed his mind.

5
Gus

The first time I saw the dolphin I was in my car, driving along the cliff road. It was early morning and the movement caught my eye. A trawler was chugging out from Carrig Cove. The dolphin was jumping in its wake. I didn't think much of it at the time – didn't know how much impact that dolphin would have on my life. The fact that there was a dolphin inside of Ross Bay did strike me as unusual, but only for a moment. I was more concerned with keeping the car on the right side of the road.

She was my first ever car, in my possession a bare twenty-four hours. That morning was my first time driving her properly. I glanced across at the passenger seat to point the dolphin out to Ferdia but the fecker was dozing. I turned my eyes back to the road and focused on safely delivering my kid brother to the bus terminal in Ballyfin in time for the 7 a.m. to Dublin. We were cutting it fine. I pressed my foot on the accelerator.

That bright blue morning everything seemed possible. Me and Ferdia weren't kids any more – I'd only one year left in school, Ferd had two. I had it all planned. Next summer, once my Leaving Cert exams were done, I wouldn't waste a single day getting out of Ross. The car was part of my escape plan and I'd washed dishes in the Bay View Hotel for the past year earning the money for it. There wasn't enough left for driving lessons. It was a good thing it was still early morning and the roads were mostly empty. A good thing too that Ferdia had conked out as soon as he'd gotten into the passenger seat or he'd have been cringing and making smart-arse remarks every time I crossed the centre line or went too close to the ditch.

Ferd's plans for exiting Ross were underway too. He'd his heart set on making the next Irish Olympic boxing team and the scholarship he'd gotten for a summer training camp in a big Dublin gym was a definite step towards achieving his goal. Truth is, when I'd put down the cash for Goldie Horn there'd been just enough left over for a few driving lessons but I'd decided to give the cash to Ferdia so he'd have some spending money in Dublin. I'd get the hang of driving soon enough. Once I dropped Ferd at the station I intended heading off on a day trip around the back roads and boreens of Donegal. I'd packed a heap of sandwiches. By the time I came back to Ross I'd be driving like an old pro.

6
Emer

The *Ella Louise* had barely chugged away from the pier that Friday morning when Rinn appeared to escort us out to sea. Dan and Jim had been a bit gruff with us when we arrived at the boat, as if they were regretting agreeing to bring us out.

'I thought there were five of ye?' Dan said as we climbed on board. 'Where's the wee lad?'

'Mam wouldn't let him come,' Fee said. 'She said he'd only be sick.'

'Right enough,' Dan said. He pointed to a small area of the trawler immediately in front of the wheelhouse where some ropes were coiled. 'You lot plant yourselves there while we cast off. No high jinks.'

'No high jinks,' Dog said, and we all moved

quickly over to the appointed place, glancing at each other but saying nothing.

Dan's mood lifted as soon as he saw the dolphin in the water. 'He's followed us out every morning so far,' he shouted, leaning out the side window as he guided the vessel towards the mouth of the bay. 'Escorts us out, hangs around us for a bit, then heads back in. You know it was the *Ella Lou* he followed into the bay in the first place?'

We nodded, craning our heads around to hear him over the din of the engine.

'We met him a few miles up the coast, near Arranmore. He stayed around for hours, then tailed us back that afternoon,' said Jim, standing half in, half out of the wheelhouse. 'We thought he'd leave once we entered the bay, but damn me if he didn't come in after us.'

'Seems to have taken a liking to our little corner of the world,' Dan said. 'Decided to stick around. For a wee while, at any rate.

'We've called him Rinn,' Dog said.

'Rinn?' Dan said. 'I like it. Suits him.'

Rinn kept pace with us as Dan manoeuvred the *Ella Lou* through the centre of the channel and headed up the coast. After an hour or so Dan stopped the boat and came out of the wheelhouse.

He indicated we could move from where he'd corralled us.

'Let's see what Rinn does now,' he said. 'This is where he usually peels off and heads back for the bay.'

We looked over the side of the trawler and for a few moments it did seem as if Rinn had vanished. The sea was quite calm – there was a breeze but it wasn't up to much.

'Yep. Fecker's buggered off,' Jim said.

'No, he hasn't,' Fee said, pointing behind us.

Head, fin, tail – he was there and gone again. A game began, us watching and waiting, Rinn appearing briefly at a different spot each time. When he got bored of that, he swam a distance away from the trawler and breached, a small leap the first time, then a much higher one, crashing back into the water in an explosion of foam. I pulled my camera from my rucksack and began shooting. The camera, a Minolta, was old as the hills. It'd been my mam's, from before she married Da, back when she'd had ideas of being a photographer. Rinn breached, I snapped. After a while he came over to the trawler. He whistled and clicked at us and flipped his snout as if he was laughing. I caught some close-ups of his face.

Jim shook his head. 'I've seen many a dolphin in

my day but I've never seen one act like this before. It's mighty peculiar.'

Dan laughed. 'Jim's theory is that Rinn's an escapee from one of those SeaWorld shows in America.' He turned his head from what he was doing and looked at me. 'Did you really swim so close you saw a scar on his face, Emer?' he said.

I nodded. 'There's scars all over him,' I said. 'He's been around, has Rinn.'

Rinn leapt and landed on his belly, sending spray into the trawler and soaking us. I had to shield the camera from the spray and as I looked down I saw the counter was at thirty-seven. I'd shot off the entire roll of film and come very close to yanking it off its spindle.

'Oh hell,' I said. 'Da'll kill me. He warned me not to use it all up.'

'Doesn't your da sell film?' Kit said. 'Can you not take as much as you want?'

Fee laughed and I shook my head. 'Da's fierce strict about using the shop as our private store. He says that's what beggars shopkeepers. Everything we use has to go in his ledger.'

'But he'd never know if you slipped a few into your pocket?' Kit said.

This brought a snort from Fee. 'Mr Monaghan

knows how many spiders there are in that shop and he charges them rent,' she said.

Dan and Jim coughed to cover their laughter.

'It's OK,' Fee said. 'Emer wasn't born yesterday. She knows exactly why her da's called Sly.'

'Because it's short for Sylvester,' Jim said, feigning innocence. 'That's why I call him Sly, anyhow.'

I joined in the laughter but I knew my face wasn't quite in it. I began fiddling with the Minolta. I rolled the film back into its casing and moved a few feet sideways as I did it.

'You OK?' Dog had moved with me. 'Do you mind?'

'Mind?' I said.

'Mind that people call him Sly, your dad,' Dog said.

I shook my head, then looked up, looked him in the eye and nodded. 'Yes,' I said. 'Yes, I do mind. Not because people call him Sly but because it fits him so well.'

'We don't choose our parents,' Dog said.

'I know,' I said. 'And Mam is great. One out of two's not bad. D'you get on OK with your mam?'

Dog nodded. 'She's a good person. She's kind of cool, you know?'

'She is,' I said. 'I love her maxi dresses.'

Deirdre Cullen was the village hippy. Younger

than most of the mams, she looked like she'd walked straight out of the photos of Woodstock. Her long hair often had flowers in it and she swished along the streets of Carrig Cove in paisley dresses or bell-bottom jeans with coloured inserts, fringed tops and chain belts. Beside her, the rest of the Carrig Cove mams, in their knitted twinsets and knee-length skirts, looked as if they were stuck permanently in 1959.

'I love her to bits,' Dog said, 'but she's too far out for the good folk of Carrig Cove. The other women are barely polite, never friendly.'

'Does it bother her?' I asked. 'Does it bother you?'

'I think it used to bother her, but only because she didn't want me being affected by it. Once she saw I had friends she let it go. She's happy growing her herbs and making her lotions and potions. I know people think she's daft with her natural cures, but she does a decent business with the health shops in Dublin and Belfast.'

'Really?' I said. 'Your mam earns money from that?'

'As opposed to taking money from the mystery man who fathered me?' Dog said, his eyes watching me carefully. 'I know there's people think she's a kept woman.'

I shook my head at him but felt my cheeks flush. A village shop is where people come to gossip and I'd heard plenty of villagers speculate about who Dog Cullen's father might be. Some said he was a wealthy guy in Galway or Dublin; some, Da included, swore Dog's father was a traveller man. All of the things I'd heard flickered through my head and I felt the consciousness of it flash across my face like neon.

'I don't mean that,' I said. 'I mean your mam has a job, she earns her own living. I think that's great. I want to do that. I don't want to be dependent on some man, like my own mam.'

I was anxious to get across what I meant, so anxious I began to wave my hands around and lost my grip on the camera which was still wide open, its fragile innards exposed. Dog caught it in the split second before it hit the deck. As he gave it back to me our fingers brushed.

'You could come and meet her sometime, my mam,' he said. 'You can have a private viewing of the maxi dresses.'

I smiled. 'I'd like that,' I said.

'Right,' said Dan. 'Enough idling. We won't even cover the cost of the diesel if we don't get moving. I think Rinn has gone fishing.' He pointed to the port side where Rinn's fin was slicing through the water, moving away from us. 'We'll shoot the net and see if he leads us through a school.'

Dan went back into the wheelhouse and Jim set to work. The net spilled out behind the stern as wc gave chase.

'Lunchtime,' Fee said, though it was barely ten o'clock. 'Anyone got interesting sandwiches? I've only got cheese.'

It was an hour before the nets were hauled in. Dan and Jim let the lads help but, to Fee's disgust, they insisted it wasn't girls' work. I sat there wishing I had another roll of film with me. Black-and-white film. I took the shots inside my head instead: a close-up of Dan's face as he concentrated on the task in hand; a wide shot of the net bursting with fish, dripping water down onto the deck; one of Jim guiding the net towards the hold; one of Kit and Dog hauling on a rope; one of Dan shouting orders; a full frame of the fish bulging against the net's diamond-shaped windows; an action shot of them spilling into the hold, still living, flickering silver; a shot of the raucous gulls circling above the boat.

An image of Dog wiping his fringe from his forehead with his forearm; a close-up of his hands holding a wriggling mackerel; a shot of him standing, legs planted firmly, one hand on his hip, the other shielding his eyes from the sun's glare; one more as he turned to look at me, smiling at me, those double dimples digging into his cheeks.

'Here's himself again,' Jim said, 'looking for what he can get.' He tossed a few tiddlers over the side. Rinn snapped up the fish before they even hit the water.

'Here,' Dan said, chucking some fish over towards Fee and myself. 'See how close he'll come.'

Fee threw her two towards Rinn, but I held mine over the edge of the boat, dangling them above the surface. Rinn ate the two Fee has tossed, then eyed mine. He approached slowly. He stopped in front of me and made some clicking sounds. Dog and the others were leaning over the side, holding their breaths, watching. Rinn and me stared at each other. I dropped one fish and he caught it. Then he reached his snout towards my hand and carefully took the mackerel right from out of my fingers.

'Will you look at that?' Jim said, and shook his head.

Now a decent catch was on board, Dan and Jim were wanting to get it back to the processing plant in Carrig as fast as possible. Fee, Kit, Dog and me were banished back to the coiled ropes in front of the wheelhouse and we set off for home. Rinn raced alongside us, surfacing constantly to watch us watching him. It was three o'clock in the afternoon when we chugged back into Ross Bay.

'It's been a great day,' Dog said. 'Thanks a million for bringing us out.

'Yes,' I said. 'It's been really special.'

'No bother,' Dan said. 'Our pleasure. Tell you what you can do though, Emer – get me a set of those photos whenever you have them developed.'

'I will,' I said.

'Uh-oh,' Jim said. 'Looks like we have a welcoming committee.'

Sure enough, there was a small crowd on the pier: Conor McNessa, most of the lads, some of the girls.

'Their noses will be out of joint,' Kit said. 'They'll have gone to the cove today to swim with Rinn and found we've up and lured him away.'

'Pity about them,' Fee said. 'We swam with him first, he's our dolphin.'

Dog and Kit sprang up to help Dan and Jim moor the boat and the older men issued orders and let the lads show off in front of the others. Fee rolled her eyes.

'Boys,' she said.

Conor was on us as soon as we climbed onto the pier. 'You lot picked the right day for getting Rinn out of town,' he said, directing these comments at Dog and Kit.

'How so?' Dog said.

'A bunch of Ross kids turned up here this morning,' Louise O'Toole said, a belligerent sneer on her face. 'That Maeve Grogan and her crowd. A whole heap of them. Thirteen, at least. They sat right in the middle of our beach, like they owned it, said they'd just come over for a swim.'

'As if they'd bother coming all the way over to swim on our bit of a beach,' Phelim Roche said, 'and they with that big white strand they're always boasting about.'

'It was obvious why they were here. They'd heard we had a dolphin and they'd come to gawk,' Mary Ryan said. 'You should have seen the faces on them when he didn't show.'

'They had this big loud conversation about how he'd probably scarpered now he's worked out what a kip Carrig Cove is,' Louise said. 'And then they decided it wasn't worth getting in for a swim over here after all.'

'That Maeve one had the cheek to say the water was probably full of fish heads from the factory,' Mary said.

'The silly bitch,' said Louise, and then sniggered to hear herself use the word. She slid her eyes sideways towards Conor, I suppose to see if her vehemence had impressed him. He smiled his easy smile and turned to Dog again.

'Didn't stop her stripping down to her bikini to work on her tan, though,' he said. He stuck out his chest and wriggled his hips and the other lads hooted. 'But seriously, Dog, you have great timing. I mean we thought that Ross lot were right and Rinn was gone. Then we saw the *Ella Louise* coming back in with him in tow. Brilliant, bloody brilliant, man.'

'Those Ross kids won't come traipsing over the causeway again,' Louise's brother JJ said. 'They'd lose too much face.'

'Yeah, Rinn's our dolphin,' Louise said. 'They can feck off.'

A chorus of yeahs seconded that. We were surrounded as we walked up the pier. Dog and Kit got all the credit for sticking it to the hated Ross kids. Fee and me were treated like appendages to the two boys, bystanders to an accidental act of sabotage.

As we walked up the street it struck me that we Carrig kids hadn't come together like this since we were little. Somewhere around eleven and twelve we'd broken up into 'the boys' and 'the girls' and then splintered into even smaller groups as we hit our teens. Yesterday we'd sort of hung out together at the beach, now here we were moving in a big gang up Main

Street. Conor and the lads swept Dog and Kit up to the front and Fee and me fell back into the middle of the girls.

Mary Ryan linked an arm through mine. 'Which of you is going with which?' she whispered.

'No one is going with anyone, Mary,' I said. 'We're hanging out together, that's all.'

'But you like Dog?' she said. 'It's just . . . well, everyone knows I've always liked Dog. But if someone else has to get him, I'd rather it was you than Fee.'

I knew that in some roundabout way Mary was killing herself trying to be nice but it irritated me that anyone thought I was out to get Dog.

'I have to go, Mary,' I said. 'We were up really early this morning and I've got to work in the shop tomorrow.'

I touched Fee's arm briefly in salute, then stepped quietly out of the little parade heading from pier to strand, and slipped away home.

7
Gus

I drove all day. I thought about crossing the border into the North but it was too good a day to risk hours queueing at a Northern Ireland customs post or getting stymied by a road closure. I stayed in Donegal, headed up towards Letterkenny and made a wide loop around the county, testing Goldie's suspension on the boreens and back roads and wincing whenever stray brambles squeaked along her paintwork.

By early afternoon I was on the road home with two hundred and forty miles added to the clock. It was hot. My head was wrecked. I needed a cigarette. I pulled over at the Hag's Finger viewing point, got out of the car and lit up. I took a long drag, leaned back against the bonnet and surveyed the bay. To my left was Ross, with its pretty Neapolitan ice-cream coloured houses, the Bay View Hotel dominating the harbour below and the church perched on the hill above.

Across the bay I could just about make out Carrig Cove if I squinted hard. Carrig Cove, grey and shabby, was where Ferd and me lived when we were kids. I knew every stone of the place, every crack in the pavement, at least those that were there when our family moved away.

We left when I was twelve and Ferd was eleven. I hadn't been back since. My mam had moved to Carrig with Da as a bride and she'd never settled. Carrig Cove was too working class for her liking and she nagged Da until he agreed to move across the bay to Ross.

But the good folk of Ross looked down their noses at Ferdia and me. We were nothing but blow-ins from the wrong side of the water. I don't think Mam ever noticed. She convinced herself that moving to Ross had been the right thing to do, the best thing, especially when Da died three years later.

The local kids had never let us in. To them we were Carrig boys. And truth told, in my heart I missed it. Six years later, I missed it. Missed my old friends. All of us – the Carrig kids and all the Ross lot – travelled to the same secondary school in Ballyfin, but the Carrig and Ross kids didn't mix. Ferd and me weren't welcome in either group so we formed our own gang of two. With Ferdia gone, I'd have to play the lone wolf.

My ciggy was done. I flicked the butt over the cliff and was about to get back in the car when I spotted the dolphin again. It rose fully out of the water, twisted in mid-air and re-entered the waves with hardly so much as a splash.

That's what I need right now, I thought. *A dip in the sea. I'll stop at Silver Strand, park Goldie and stroll down the beach, swinging my car keys.*

8

Gus

The beach was heaving. Half of Ross must have been there but I didn't bother looking around me. I stripped down to my swimming trunks and walked straight into the water the way Da taught us. *No messing around,* he'd say. *Don't think about the cold. Splash a little water on the back of your neck to prepare you for the shock, then one-two-three, down.*

I swam out, straight out, beyond all the other swimmers, just like the water safety ads say not to. I swam till I was almost bolloxed, then turned and came back to shore. As I walked back to my stuff I heard someone call my name through the din of screeching kids and tinny transistor music.

'Hey Gus.'

I scanned the bodies splayed on the sand.

‘It is Gus, right? Gus McRoy?’ A hand was held out to mine. It belonged to a guy called Ali Matthews. He was sitting on a deckchair, shading his eyes from the sun and smiling up at me. His girlfriend, Maeve Grogan, was lying beside him on a lilo, stretched out on her front. She twisted her head to acknowledge me and raised a hand in salute.

This is a first, I thought. Maeve and Ali, the undisputed queen and king of the Ross crowd, had never deigned to notice me before.

‘Got yourself a car, I see,’ Ali said.

‘I did,’ I said.

‘Nice,’ he said. ‘Pity about the colour.’

‘I like yellow,’ Maeve said. She rolled over on the lilo, shading her eyes with a hand as she looked up at me. ‘It’s my favourite colour.’

There were plenty of pretty girls swishing around Ross but pretty wasn’t the word for Maeve Grogan. Beautiful was more like it. Spectacularly beautiful. Elizabeth Taylor, Brigitte Bardot kind of beautiful. Maeve had it all – the eyes, the face, the hair, the body. The body. Ohmygod, the body. I’d gotten an eyeful as she rolled over. Three days of sunshine had everyone in Ireland turned various shades of tomato but Maeve Grogan was an even golden-brown. She was wearing a lemon-yellow bikini, little triangles of material held together with golden rings, one ring at each hip and another between her breasts. She'd undone the strings at her neck and now she sat up to retie them. She curled her legs under her and patted the lilo.

'Sit,' she said.

I hesitated. I considered walking away to show them I wasn't flattered by their sudden attention. Thing is, I was.

'Sit here,' Ali said. He slid off the deckchair onto the lilo beside Maeve. I sat in the chair. Ali produced a pack of Players. I took one and he lit it for me.

'Carrig Cove,' Maeve said, taking her long hair in one hand and arranging it over her left shoulder. 'Tell us about Carrig Cove, Gus.' Ali rested a hand on Maeve's thigh. They both looked up at me expectantly.

'Why?' I asked.

'It's right over there.' Ali twisted his head around to indicate the other side of the bay. 'Been there all our lives, but we really don't know much about it.'

'What do you want to know?' I asked.

'Everything,' Maeve said. 'Anything. What age were you and your brother when you left?'

'We were kids,' I said. 'I was twelve, Ferdia was eleven.'

Ali said, 'And why did your family move?'

'My mam had notions,' I said. 'She thought Carrig Cove was too working class for her family – she's originally from Ballyfin. She thought Ferdia and me were getting common accents and we'd have a better future if we moved somewhere more posh. Better accents and a better address for future job interviews.' I curled my lip.

'Your mammy was right,' Maeve said. 'It mightn't matter to us, but the world out there' – she indicated the landmass of Ireland behind us with her hands – 'it cares. It cares very much. Your mammy just wants what's best for you, like every Irish mammy.'

'The people in Carrig Cove are the salt of the earth,' I said.

'I'm sure they are,' Maeve said, 'as long as all you want from life is to be a fisherman. And I think you want more than that for yourself, Gus McRoy.' She smiled at me.

'That guy, Dog,' Ali said. 'He didn't actually kill a dog, did he?'

'He did,' I said. 'A feckin' huge Rottweiler, it was too. Killed it with a hurley and sliotar. I was there – I saw him do it.' This wasn't strictly true – the dog was already dead when I turned up – but that didn't matter now.

'Lucky shot,' Ali said.

I shook my head. 'Dog plays minors for the county, wing forward. The seniors are hoping that when he joins them next year they'll have a decent crack at the Ulster Championship.'

'I don't follow the GAA,' Ali said, shrugging. 'More a rugby guy myself.'

'You play hurling, Gus, don't you?' Maeve said. 'You and Ferdia?'

Maeve Grogan knew I played hurling? I tried not to let my surprise show. I nodded. 'I used to. I was pretty good but no match for Dog. Ferdia was talented but he gave it up to concentrate on boxing. Dog did the opposite, gave up boxing for hurling.'

'So, your brother is a better fighter than Dog Cullen?' Ali said.

'Right now I'd say Dog is his equal. Most people would say that. But Ferdia has gone to train in one of the best gyms in Dublin for the summer. I'm thinking when he comes back no one around here will have the beating of him, not even Dog.'

'Ferdia and Dog must have been in competition with each other a lot,' Maeve said. 'And you too. Is that why you never go back there? Too hard to stay friends?'

I frowned. *How did she know that I never went back?* 'We're still friends, Dog and me,' I said. 'We're in a few classes together in school. We used to do hurley practice together till I gave it up. We still hang out.' As I said it I realised that wasn't really true. I hadn't spoken to Dog in ages, other than to nod hello across a room. Now I'd gotten too old to play for the minors I barely saw him at all.

'But you never go back over to Carrig Cove?' Maeve insisted. 'Why?'

I shrugged. 'Nothing there for me any more, nor Ferd neither. Our lives are here.'

'No other friends over there? What about that Conor McNessa guy?' she said.

'He's an arse,' I said, unable to keep the animosity out of my voice.

'Oooo!' Maeve sat forward, pulled her knees into her body and rested her chin in her hands. She hadn't taken her green eyes off me since I'd sat down in the deckchair. Ali was watching me intently too. I felt like the chief witness in a murder trial.

What do they want from me? I should have asked them straight out. I should have stood up and walked away, but Maeve's eyes had me pinned in that chair and truth is, I liked it. I'd spent six years watching Maeve Grogan, staring at her when I thought she wasn't looking. The view from that deckchair made it easy to ignore the feeling that somehow I was walking into a snare.

'Conor McNessa is an arse, is he?' Maeve said. 'I smell a story. Do tell.'

'It's nothing,' I said. 'Kid stuff. We rub each other up the wrong way, is all.'

'No matter,' she said. 'I'll just wait till Ferdia is back and make him tell me.' She laughed her tinkly mocking laugh, leaned back on her elbows, raised her face to the sun and closed her eyes. 'It'll be better coming from him anyway. Baby brothers always love telling tales on their big brothers – he'll give me the interesting bits you'll leave out.'

She had me there. Better to tell the miserable little story myself than let Ferdia do it.

'It's really nothing,' I said, aware that my efforts to keep my voice light sounded forced. 'Kid stuff, like I said. "Who's-the-King-of-the-Castle" stuff. I was the oldest kid in our gang in Carrig, nearly a year older than everyone else, so I was *it* – the leader, top dog.'

'You were top dog, not Dog Cullen?' Ali asked. Maeve laughed.

'Dog's always been separate,' I said. 'He's friends with everyone, but he's not really part of the mob. He never tries to lead it – doesn't follow either. Dog does his own thing.'

'So you were Alpha boy,' Maeve said. 'I can see

that, big strapping lad like you. What happened? Conor topple your crown?'

'Something like that,' I said. 'It's not what he did so much as the way he did it.' I flicked my dead cigarette away into the dunes behind us. 'Once Ferdia and me knew we were leaving Carrig Cove we told everyone. We were devastated to be going, and to Ross of all places.'

Ali and Maeve grinned and nodded. The enmity between Carrig Cove and Ross went back generations.

'Conor and me had become close and that last year he'd been like my lieutenant, or something. I knew that when we moved he'd take over the gang. They'd be his. But Conor couldn't wait, could he?'

'Ah, treachery!' Maeve said. She was sitting up again, watching me, her eyes doing a half-teasing, half-sympathetic dance only a girl like her could get away with. 'What did he do?'

'There were still two months to go before we moved to Ross but that's forever when you're that age. Conor took me aside one day and said he had this idea, something that would bind all of us lads together so nothing would change when we left.'

'Dramatic!' Maeve said. 'I thought only little girls did the "let's be friends forever and ever and ever" rubbish.'

'Boys' friendships are just as strong,' Ali said. 'We just swallow it when stuff goes wrong. Girls are always taking offence and making a drama of everything.'

'Some girls do,' Maeve said. 'Some girls don't. Go on, Gus. What happened?'

'He told me the gang would be meeting at the old barn up in Delaney's field, our usual spot for a pow wow, and we should be there at three the next day, me and Ferdia. So we went, and all the lads were there, except for Dog. He was off winning some competition – poetry or storytelling, I can't remember. Conor would never have done what he did if Dog had been around.

'Anyway, the boys made a circle with me and Ferdia in the centre, like we were guests of honour. Conor said we were going to become blood brothers. He handed out a couple of blades he'd nicked from his da's razor.

'Everyone got real quiet. Conor told us to cut ourselves on the pad of both thumbs. Jesus. I don't know how one of us didn't bleed out or end up with gangrene. We passed the blades around. Once we'd cut our thumbs we were to press them to the thumbs of the lads on either side of us. The others were in a circle so that left Ferdia and me to press our thumbs to each other's, which didn't make much sense since we were actual brothers. I thought about pointing it out to Conor but I didn't like to interfere – after all he'd planned this specially for me.

'Then he said we were going to swear a special oath. He would read it out one line at time and we were to say it after him.'

'Uh-oh,' Ali said.

'Yeah,' I said. 'It started out fine – friends forever, we'd always have each other's backs, blah, blah. The sinker was in the last couple of lines, I can't remember the exact words . . .'

'Bet you can,' Ali said.

'"We, the boys of Carrig Cove, stand united against our enemy – the town of Ross." That got a cheer. And then, "We reserve our deepest darkest hatred for those amongst us who defect to the enemy; they shall be outcasts forever." Ferd and me had the words repeated before I took them in. Suddenly everyone's eyes were on Ferd and me, watching us like we were rats in a cage. They looked to Conor as if they were waiting for a signal. I grabbed Ferdia's arm and we ran like the hounds of hell, burst through the circle and got ourselves back home as fast as we could.'

'Jesus,' Maeve said. 'It's like that story they make us do in school – what's it called?'

'*Lord of the Rings*,' Ali said.

'*Lord of the Flies*, you prize thick. And Gus was Fatty.'

I felt my cheeks redden. 'Stupid kid stuff,' I said. 'It doesn't matter, but I couldn't understand why Conor did it. He was going to be the leader when I was gone – why couldn't he wait?'

'You really can't see why?' Ali said.

I blinked at him. 'And you can?'

'Of course. He didn't want to succeed to leader-of-the-gang position by default. And he was right – it's a weak way to take over. He needed to win the leadership from you, take it while you were still there.'

Maeve nodded. 'I can see why you called him an arse, Gus. He is, but a cunning arse, you've got to give him that.'

'Says the girl who knows a cunning arse when she sees one.' Ali laughed and pulled her towards him. They wrestled for a moment and then he kissed her. They were right in front of me, so close that my shadow was covering the both of them like a purple cloak. She caught my eye over his shoulder, caught my eye and held it. When Ali made to pull away she pulled him back and kissed him again. And the whole time she was kissing him – her lips pressed hard against his, her fingers in his hair – the whole time, Maeve Grogan was looking at me, and her eyes were laughing.

9
Emer

On Saturday Carrig Cove got its first taste of dolphin fever. Cars, as many as thirty, made their way along the cliff road and cut across the causeway. Every car disgorged a family in shorts and sandals, and every family headed straight to the beach. They'd heard about Rinn and had come to swim with him.

The shop was busy all day, between the visitors coming in looking for ice cream, and locals coming in to discuss the visitors. By the afternoon it was sweltering outside and the shop was stuffy. Da was like a fractious child, unable to decide whether to be delighted by this unexpected extra business or cross at being taken off guard by it. He fixed an ingratiating smile on his face for the new customers and took his irritation out on me. I longed to be on the beach with the sun on my skin and the cold sea a few feet away. I longed to be with Dog.

'What was it like on the beach?' I asked Fee when she came into the shop later.

'It was weird,' Fee said. 'I mean, when have you ever seen people come over here to swim on our weeny beach? I heard one snotty cow complaining about the colour of the sand.' Fee pulled a snooty face and put on her best posh accent: '"Look at it, Dermot, it's *grey*!"'

'Well, it's not the Silver Strand, that's for sure,' I said. The beach near Ross was like the beaches you see in films, fine white sand and big billowy dunes. In good weather it was a magnet for families from Ballyfin and Cluain. Occasionally a car strayed across the causeway to Carrig Cove but they never stayed long.

'Well, I'm sure Silver Strand was jammers today,' Fee said. 'Ireland thinks it's the Costa-del-fecking-Sol this month.' She examined a patch of sunburn on her shoulder. 'My freckles are joining together,' she said. 'You're gorgeous and golden and I look like a flipping Dalmatian.'

'How'd they all hear about Rinn anyway?' I said. 'It's not even a week since he arrived.'

'I'd say it was the younger kids talking in school,'

Fee said. Carrig Cove kids travelled to school in Ballyfin and the primary schools weren't closed for the summer yet, not for another few weeks.

Fee stood to one side for a minute to let me serve Mrs Ryan. Da was busy arguing with a woman from Ballyfin who was trying to get him to buy back the bucket and spade set she'd bought her toddler earlier in the day.

'He has one exactly like it at home,' she said. 'I only bought this set because we forgot to bring it. He's used it once – you can take something off for that. The sand you have here is useless for making castles anyway. You really have no business selling buckets and spades at all.'

Fee choked. 'Jesus,' she whispered. 'Your da has met his match.'

'She won't get her money back, just the same,' I said.

Sure enough, Da sent the woman packing with a flea in her ear and the unwanted bucket and spade still in her hands.

'Good for you, Sylvester,' Mrs Ryan said. 'Never heard the like. I doubt she'd try that on in one of the shops in Ballyfin.'

Da came back to the register and I fetched the sweeping brush to tidy up for closing.

'Anyway,' Fee said, keeping pace as I swept, 'the beach was crazy. Conor and the lads got in with Rinn to show the visitors how it's done. The visitors watched for about five seconds, then the whole lot of them piled in. Well, the daddies did, and the bigger kids. Most of the mammies stayed in the shallows with the wee ones.'

'What did Rinn do?' I asked.

'He was OK at first, because no one went too close. Then one daddy swam right out and tried to grab his fin. I suppose he thought Rinn'd tow him around like the dolphin on *Flipper*.'

'Crikey. What happened?'

'Rinn flicked him off and Conor and co had to go in and help him out of the water. You should have seen the man's face. He was mortified. Snapped the head off his poor wife when she tried to check him for wounds.'

'Were Dog and Kit not there?' I asked, glancing over to make sure Da wasn't listening.

'They were playing a match this morning. They came late,' she said. 'And I said to them, well that's it, we'll never get near Rinn again, and Kit said . . . you'll never guess what he said?'

'Probably not,' I said, 'so just tell me.'

She crouched down in the aisle as if whispering

wasn't enough for what she was about to tell. 'Kit, he said, let's us four – you, me, him and Dog – go swimming at night, when there's no one else there.' She pulled back to watch my reaction.

'At night?' I hissed. 'Swimming at night?'

'Midnight. Sneak out and go to the beach. Us four. What do you think?'

'You're mad,' I whispered. 'I think you've lost your marbles, Fedelma Hennessy.'

'But you'll come?' she said.

I began sweeping again, away from her. She let me go, waiting for me to think it through.

I thought, *I can't!*

I thought, *But, oh, I want to.*

I thought, *If I think about this too much I won't do it.*

I swept back towards Fee.

'Yes,' I whispered as I turned past her into the next aisle. 'Yes, I'll come.'

10

Emer

I knew sneaking out of my house at midnight wouldn't be difficult, at least not in theory. My room was on the ground floor, behind the shop. I only had to lift my bedroom window and slide across the sill into the yard. From there I could slip along the side passage and though the side gate, into the street.

Slide, slip, creep, I thought. *That's all you have to do. No problem. Think how much harder it will be for Fee.*

Fee's bedroom was upstairs, slap bang between her parents and Rory. She'd have to negotiate at least three creaky spots on the stairs and then open and close the front door without anyone hearing her. I knew Fee would relish the danger. For Fee this whole thing was an adventure, something to take her another step away from childhood and towards breaking free of her ma. Me, I liked to take my steps towards adulthood slowly – careful measured steps. But that night I was as excited as I was scared.

You can do this, Emer Monaghan, I thought, as my heart span in my chest. *Stay calm and think of Rinn.*

But Rinn wasn't the only magnet drawing me out of my bed that night. I wanted to see Dog, to see the night on his skin. Darkness would make everything different and new.

Da was always in bed by ten because he had to be up on time for the paper and milk deliveries. He expected Mam and me to go to bed early too, but on Saturdays we'd sometimes stay up to watch a film, if there was one on. That night there was an old Fred and Ginger musical. I told Mam I was too tired to watch it and she looked surprised but said she wouldn't bother with it so. She went up after Da. I'd been counting on her doing that and felt bad about it, but if I was going to do this I definitely needed both my parents in bed and asleep.

I tried to read a book until it was time to go, but I didn't take in a word of it. My mind was already out there on the beach. When my watch showed ten to twelve I went over to the window.

'That's one small step for woman, one giant leap for me,' I whispered, and slid out the window.

It was balmy, like every night had been this past week, but I was shivering. Maybe it was the cut-off jeans. I'd decided to put them on for the first time and I felt self-conscious in them. I tugged the frayed edges down my thighs and peeked out the side gate before I went through it. It was unlikely the drinkers outside Paudy's would notice me all the way over here in the dark but I didn't want to bump into someone heading home early from their last pint. I hugged the houses, tiptoeing like a thief. Fee had arranged to meet me at the turn to Hill Street. We didn't say a word, just burst into nervous giggles.

'Shush, shush,' Fee hissed.

'Shush, you,' I said.

We linked arms like we used to when we were little girls and dashed across the road and through the entrance to the beach. The streetlights that ran along the wall spilled some of their light onto the sand. Dog and Kit were already there. No one would hear us on the beach but we whispered anyway – *Hi, hi, hi. Anyone see you? No, you? No. Let's go* – and then we were down to our swimsuits and rushing to the water. We took one another's hands at the edge, like we did the first day. Six days ago. Forever ago.

'What if he's asleep?' Fee said.

'Do dophins sleep?' Kit asked.

We all thought about that one for a minute but none of us knew the answer.

'Let's call him,' Dog said.

He let go my hand and began to slap the surface of the water with flat palms. We did the same. Nothing happened so we gave up and began to swim, staying together, moving slowly through the black water. No one spoke. We were breathless with being out in the night under the stars while the village behind us lay still and unaware. Suddenly Rinn was there, quietly coming up alongside us.

Hello. You called me and I came.

We greeted him, treading water as he circled. He whistled a few times but there was no fuss, no darting around. Maybe we only imagined that he recognised us, knew us for the first people he'd befriended. He came near, quite near, to all four of us, but mostly to me. He only stayed a short while. When he swam away I watched him as long as I could make out the dark fin rising in the waves.

'Where does he go?' I said.

No one answered. I looked around. Fee and Kit were already wading back to the beach. It was just Dog and me in the water. The night looked good on him, as I'd known it would.

'That was the best,' I said. I sounded out of breath. 'Don't you think?'

'Better than the boat trip?' Dog asked.

'Yeah,' I said. 'Something about it being dark makes it special.'

Dog nodded. He was very close; his legs brushed mine in the water. 'I agree,' he said, and he leaned forward and kissed me.

One quick salt-flavoured kiss.

'Come on,' he said.

We swam back to shore. He took my hand as we walked out of the water. He pulled me towards him and kissed me again, an altogether different kiss.

My body pressed against his, wet skin to wet skin.

A hand in my hair, a hand on my hip.

My hands on his skin, his back, his neck.

Lips, soft lips, warm wet lips, salty-sweet lips.

His tongue parting my lips.

My tongue, his tongue, my tongue, his tongue.

You taste me. I taste you.

I taste you tasting me.

We kissed and kissed and kissed until I began to shiver. Dog put his arm around my shoulders then and we walked up the beach.

Fee and Kit sprang apart as we approached them and we all laughed. We dressed quickly and headed back to the road, me hand-in-hand with Dog, Fee hand-in-hand with Kit.

'So,' Kit said. 'Fee and I have decided. We're coming again tomorrow. And every night. This is going to be our time with Rinn.'

'No one else, just us,' Fee said. 'Us four.'

Dog looked at me. I nodded.

'Us four,' he said.

When we got to the turn to Hill Street, Kit went with Fee and Dog kept walking with me, all the way back to the shop. We kissed again in the shadows by the side gate.

'See you tomorrow night, Emer Monaghan,' Dog whispered, tweaking a strand of my hair.

'Tomorrow night, Dog Cullen,' I said.

He waited as I slipped through the gate. When I was inside my room, lowering the window down behind me I heard him move away, back towards Hill Street.

11
Emer

Da opened the shop for a few hours on Sunday mornings so people could buy their newspapers after mass and morning service. That Sunday, around twelve-thirty when we'd normally close up, cars started arriving. More visitors coming to see Rinn. Da announced that we'd stay open for the rest of the day.

'They'll be needing ice cream in this heat,' he said, as if keeping the shop open was an act of charity on his part.

'What about our dinner?' Mam said. 'It'll be ruined.'

'We can eat it cold,' Da said. 'It's too hot for a roast today anyway.'

Mam raised her eyebrows in my direction and I smothered a laugh.

'I thought salads were only fit for rabbits?' Mam said. 'That's what you said the last time I suggested one.'

'Humph,' Da said. He went back to reorganising the ice-cream fridge, which was a mess from the day before.

'What's happening over there?' Mam said, going to stand in the doorway.

At first I couldn't see what she meant; it looked like any other Sunday morning to me. Dan and Jim, Patsy Roche and Mickser McCabe, Martin Cox, Old Willie Henry, Tom and Ben Fitz, standing around on the pier in their Sunday best, yabbering. A longer look told me Mam was right – there was something going on. The men were agitated, Mickser was pacing, voices were raised, no one was laughing.

'They're probably arguing about whether or not Ireland should have joined the EEC,' I said.

Mam shook her head. 'It's more than that,' she said. She tugged me out onto the footpath. Words floated across to us: 'Eating all our fish . . . do something . . . bloody nuisance . . . cars all over the place . . . no end of trouble . . .'

Rinn. They were talking about Rinn. I looked at Mam.

'Go on,' she said. 'Go over and find out what they're at.'

I ran across the road towards the pier and stopped about fifteen feet away from the men, close enough to hear what was being said.

'It's only one dolphin,' Dan was saying, 'not a whole damn pod. Why are ye fussing over one piddling dolphin? Save your worrying for those blasted illegal trawlers sneaking into our grounds from Holland and France, why don't you?'

'What's going on?' Da appeared at my shoulder, making me jump.

'They're having a row over the dolphin,' I said, expecting Da to roll his eyes and tell me to get back to the shop.

'What about it?' he said.

'They're saying he'll take all the fish and Dan is saying he won't.'

Da frowned. He pulled his shop coat off and handed it to me. 'Hold that,' he said. He ran his fingers through his thinning hair, pulled a smile across his face and stepped over to join the group of men. I was surprised. Da always kept well out of any local squabbles for fear that by siding with one customer he'd offend another. Mam came running over to me and grabbed the shop coat.

'Go after him,' she said. 'I'll look after the shop.' She gave me a small push and I didn't need telling again.

'. . . wreck our livelihoods, Dan,' Martin Cox was saying as I came up to the group and stopped behind Da, who was standing on the edge of the ring of men. 'The kids may think it's a lark having a dolphin lepping around the bay but we know better.'

This got a chorus of aye-ayes.

'It's my livelihood as much as yours,' Dan said, 'and I say live and let live. It's a wild animal, and you know what? The kids are right – it is a fine thing to have it hanging around for a while. It'll get bored soon enough and be away off with itself.'

'I dunno, Dan,' Willie Henry said. 'I think it likes it here. It's found itself a cushy number, hasn't it? Maybe someone's feeding it their discards, eh?'

Dan scowled. 'D'you think I was born yesterday, Willie Henry? I know better than to treat a wild animal like a pet.'

'Then let us get rid of it and be done arguing,' Patsy said.

Rid of it? What did he mean? He couldn't mean . . . I opened my mouth to protest but Da shot me a keep-quiet-and-leave-it-to-the-men glare. I bit my lip. Inside I was boiling but I knew if I broke out and spoke my mind right then and there they'd laugh at me, tell me to whisht, maybe even pat me on the head.

Wait, I told myself. *Play it cool. Choose the right moment.*

'I'll not stand by and see it killed,' Dan said. 'If it's not gone by this day next week I'll drive it off myself.'

'And how do you plan on doing that? Wasn't it you it followed in here in the first place?' Mickser McCabe said, his voice equal parts cigarette smoke and sarcasm. 'It'll think you're taking it for a day trip and be back in here after you, like a pet poodle.'

'Give me a week,' Dan said. 'I'll figure something out.' He spotted me lurking behind Da and said, 'You lot know it's illegal to kill dolphins, right? Now Ireland has thrown its lot in with Europe no one can go around killing anything without a licence.'

'And who's going to know what we do?' Mickser said. 'Who'll tell?'

'Me,' I said, loud and steady. 'I'll tell.'

This silenced the lot of them. I expected Da to bawl me out of it. A vein popped on his forehead but he said nothing.

'And will you be letting her, Sly?' Patsy asked. 'Because it wouldn't sit well with anyone here if you did.'

Da cleared his throat. 'No daughter of mine will be snitching on her own people, that's certain. But if you don't mind me saying so I think you're being a bit hasty.'

'I don't take your meaning, Sly,' Mickser growled. He plucked the spent cigarette from between his teeth, stabbed the butt onto the pier wall, then ground it under his shoe for good measure. I watched a trickle of sweat roll down the back of Da's neck. His smile widened into a grimace.

'Well,' he said, 'I'm thinking there's money to be made from our marine visitor and it seems a right shame to kill a goose before it lays a single egg.'

A few of the men exchanged looks and one or two made tsk, tsk sounds under their breath.

'I see the way of it,' Patsy Roche said. 'It doesn't matter if we're losing half our catch so long as Sly Monaghan is raking it in on ice creams and lemonade for the sightseers.'

'I won't deny I made some money yesterday,' Sly said. 'And I hope to make some more today. Sure and wouldn't everyone like some easy money in these hard times?'

'We can have the cloud and you'll cash in the silver lining, is that it?' Martin Cox said.

'No,' Da said, drawing it out so it sounded more like a maybe. 'The way I see it, this situation could be win, win, for everyone.'

'What do you mean?' Dan said.

'I mean I see opportunities here that could benefit the whole village,' Da said, waving his hands about to indicate the group of men, the boats, the shops, the pub. 'The other day you and Jim took this lassie' – he pointed at me – 'and some of her pals out on the *Ella Louise*, and the dolphin followed you out and jumped around a bit. Herself and her pals came back only delighted with themselves. They'd had a fine day out and had a real once-in-a-lifetime experience. Wouldn't you say, Emer?'

I nodded.

'Jaysus, I've seen it all now,' Tom Fitz said. 'Sly Monaghan, animal lover.'

The men laughed and Da laughed along, as if he hadn't heard the scorn in Tom's voice.

'My point is,' he said, 'if Dan here had charged the kids for the trip he'd be a few quid better off. The people turning up here this weekend might like to take a trip like that, only shorter and minus the fish.'

'Come off it,' Patsy said. 'Who in their right mind would pay to see a damned dolphin?'

'Folk who've never seen one in real life, Patsy,' Dan said. 'Look at how many are turning up right now on the off chance of catching sight of him in the water. We got right close to him on the *Ella Lou*. He put on a show for us out there, didn't he, Emer?'

I nodded. 'Just like *Flipper* on the telly,' I said. 'Lots of people would pay for that. I bet they would. Sixty pence for adults, thirty pence per child, one pound fifty for a family ticket.'

'The apple doesn't fall far from the tree, eh Sly?' Dan said. He winked at me.

Da, who had manoeuvred his way to Dan's right side while he was speaking, smiled weakly. No one had ever suggested I resembled him before.

'There's none of you fishing more than half the week,' Da said. 'Ye can't compete with them big European trawlers. Your boats can't make it out to Rockall or the Porcupine Bank where all the decent fishing is. I'm betting you could earn more from a boatload of tourists than a boatload of cod. Easy money, it'd be.'

'Are you seriously suggesting we abandon fishing to run day trips?' Martin said. I noticed he sounded more curious than incredulous.

'No,' Da said. 'I'm suggesting you consider forming some sort of co-op between you. Half the boats stay fishing, half do the day trips, split the work between ye and split the profits.'

The men stared.

'Several short trips out into the bay every day, instead of trying to scrounge a living inshore fishing,'

Da said. 'Nice sociable hours, no heavy lifting, and you'd not be risking your lives doing it neither. And the visitors will be wanting food and drink, and ice creams and lemonade and film for their cameras. Some of them may even want to stay around for a few days. I think this is a fine opportunity for our village so I'm with Dan. I say we should try and keep the animal here, not get rid of it.'

'But how do we get people to come?' was the next question.

'Aren't they coming already?' Dan said. 'And that's just word of mouth.'

'Don't worry about that end of things,' Da said. 'Emer took a heap of photos the other day. We'll send them to the local papers. We'll make posters. You provide the boats, I'll make sure you have customers.'

'And what if the dolphin goes and buggers off?' Mickser said.

'Eh?' Dan said. His bushy eyebrows shot skywards in mock surprise. 'Five minutes ago you wanted to club the creature to death, now you're worried about it leaving?'

'I'm just saying—'

'We'll cross that bridge if we come to it,' Da said. 'Right now I say we should make hay while the sun shines.' He pointed up at the perfect blue sky. 'We have weather the like of which we've never seen and a dolphin who seems to have chosen to spend the summer with us. Gift horse, I say, gift horse. And I for one don't intend looking it in the mouth.'

'Why don't we all head over to Paudy's and discuss this, glass in hand?' Dan said, pulling at his shirt and flapping the cotton against his chest. 'I could murder a pint.'

This got general approval from the rest of the men and the whole group began to shuffle across the road towards the pub.

'Look after the shop,' Da said to me. 'And make sure that roll of film you took is ready to send off to be processed first thing in the morning, there's a good girl.'

I nodded and headed back to the shop, stunned. Da, who never went drinking in Paudy's, was going there and on a Sunday, no less. Stunned that the other men had wanted to kill Rinn and that Da, of all people, was the one who'd figured out a way to save him.

'You know it's all about the money?' Fee said later, when I told her what'd happened. 'He'd have been for killing Rinn if the only way to make cash out of him was dolphin steaks.'

I pulled a face at her. 'Doesn't matter, as long as

Rinn is safe,' I said. 'I'm certain sure we'd have been waking up tomorrow to his body on the beach if Dan and Da hadn't come up with a plan.'

'A plan that's going to turn Carrig Cove on its head,' Fee said. 'This is certainly going to be one interesting summer.'

II

12
Gus

I'd been counting on getting more hours in the hotel that summer but things were slow in Ross, despite the good weather. The dolphin I'd seen in the bay had attached itself to Carrig Cove and everyone was heading straight past Ross and across the causeway to take trips on dolphin boats. I was tickled that the wee village of Carrig Cove had finally got one over on Ross but I wasn't so happy when Hannibal, the head cook at the Bay View, told me he didn't need me on Thursday. Thursday was one of my regular nights.

'But I'm here now,' I said. 'Are you sure you can't let me have an hour or two?'

Hannibal shook his massive head. 'Sorry, Gus,' he said. 'The dining room is practically empty and there's no other bookings. I'll ring you tomorrow if I need you.'

'But tomorrow's Friday,' I said. 'I always do Friday.'

He shrugged and went back into the kitchen, letting the door to the yard slap shut in my face.

'It's that damn fish,' said a voice behind me – Maeve Grogan's voice.

'The dolphin?' I said, turning to her. She was leaning against the wall, looking amused. Maeve always looked amused, as if the whole world had been arranged the way it was especially for her entertainment. 'Dolphins are mammals,' I said, 'not fish.'

'I was being sarcastic,' she said, raising an eyebrow. 'One way or other, the thing is bad for business.'

'Ross business,' I said. 'Great for Carrig Cove.'

'Ah,' she said, catching the bias in my voice. 'Still a Carrig boy under the skin. Well, it's cost you tonight. If the hotel isn't doing business then gorgeous Gus might be out of a job.'

She was standing right in front of me now, looking up at me, past my eyes to the top of my head, as if she was lost in judging my height. She moved nearer until there was barely an inch between our bodies. I could feel her breath on my skin, could feel her heat.

'You're a beautiful boy, Gus McRoy.' She ran a

hand along my forearm. 'You make all the Ross boys look like runts.'

'All?' I said.

She laughed. 'Even Ali looks a bit on the short side next to you. He's mad jealous, you know. He's always claiming to be six foot, but he's half an inch shy. What height are you, anyway? Six three?'

'Six four,' I said.

She dropped her gaze to my eyes, laughed at my confusion and stepped away. 'Would you like the tour?' she said.

'What?'

'The tour. Of the hotel. You've probably never been beyond the kitchens, have you?'

I shook my head. 'I haven't,' I said.

'Come on, then,' she said. She pushed open the door Hannibal had just shut in my face. 'Come.' She reached into the yard, grabbed my hand and tugged. I let her pull me back inside. Hannibal and the other men looked up from their work and looked away again when they saw I was with Maeve.

Maeve Grogan, the boss's daughter. Her dad, Aidan Grogan, owned the Bay View. He was the wealthiest man for miles around, handsome, successful, and, according to those who did business with him, an arrogant shite. As a lowly kitchen hand I had no dealings with him. He floated around Ross in a silver Merc, like he owned the whole place. Which he did, pretty much. Besides the Bay View there were a couple of properties on Church Street, a newsagent's and a pub called The Cruachan. A lot of the kids in Ross came from middle-class families with daddies who had jobs in the companies and industries in Ballyfin. Money wasn't flush but nowhere as tight as it was in our house or in the houses over in Carrig. Maeve's family was proper wealthy and so was Ali Matthews's.

'You know the kitchen already,' Maeve said, walking straight through, pulling me behind her. She shoved the doors to the dining room open. The only diners, a couple at the window table, glanced up; Maeve ignored at them. We went out into the foyer where the woman on the front desk quickly sat up straight and tried to hide the book she was reading. Maeve nodded to her and walked lightly up the stairs. I followed in her wake like a shadow unsure of its angle. At the top we turned into a corridor. A brown carpet splashed with huge orange flowers ran ahead of us and large paintings of local beauty spots hung along the cream walls, filling the spaces between the doors.

'Let's see,' Maeve said, trailing her free hand from

wall to door to wall to door to wall to door. 'Number seventeen. This will do.' She threw the door open and walked inside. I followed her as far as the threshold.

'Don't be shy,' she said. Her eyes were mocking me again. *What was she up to? Was I being tricked?* I didn't know what to think. I didn't want to think. I walked in and she walked back towards me, reached around me and shut the door. And locked it. She was up against me now and I automatically put a hand to her hip.

'Word has it that you have an enormous cock, Gus McRoy,' she said. 'Is it true?'

My cheeks flamed. I didn't know where to look, so I looked straight at her. She was fiddling with the buttons on the front of her flowery dress. I glanced back at the door.

'Don't fret about us being disturbed,' she said. 'My father turns a blind eye. He'd rather I use a room than the back seat of a car.'

'Your da knows you . . .'

'Have sex? Well, it's like this: Daddy darling is no saint. He has a harem – my mother, a long-term girlfriend in Sligo, an occasional one in Belfast, and whatever floozies he happens to encounter on his travels. I don't lick it off the stones and he knows it. As long as I'm discreet I think he rather likes it that

I'm not your usual wee milk-and-water Catholic girl, crossing her legs and saying a decade of the rosary.'

'What about Ali?' I said.

'What about him?' she said.

'I don't like . . .' I fumbled for words because the truth is I couldn't stand Ali Matthews. I thought he was a smarmy stuck-up git and I relished the idea of getting one over on him.

'I'm the one doing the cheating here,' Maeve said. 'If I don't care, why should you?'

She let her dress fall off her shoulders to the floor and there was no more protesting from me. I couldn't shed my own clothes fast enough. She grabbed my face in her hands the way she'd grabbed Ali's that afternoon on the beach a few weeks ago, but this time her lips were on my lips, and I was kissing her back, not just watching and wishing.

13

Gus

It was one o'clock in the morning when we left the hotel. I offered to walk her home but Maeve shook her head.

'There's no one around to see,' I said.

'Ali may turn up. He does sometimes. Comes around throwing pebbles at my window. He says he's being romantic but we both know he's checking up on me, making sure I'm home in my bed.'

'What if he's already there?'

'I've been for a walk, haven't I? He knows better than to push it.' She raked her fingers through her hair, pulling it back into order. 'You can walk me as far as the split in the road,' she said, linking her arm through mine. 'I want to ask you something anyway, a favour. It's not for me, it's for Ned Cranny and Ratty McRoth.'

'Why would I want to do a favour for those bozos?' I said.

'Because they're my friends,' she said. 'And I'm your friend and that makes them your friends too.' Her voice was light but the look in her eyes told me I was being tested. She was opening the way to her inner circle for me, the circle I'd been left out of ever since coming to Ross. I could tell I needed to step in or step out.

'OK,' I said. 'What do they want?'

'They are mad to see that dolphin in Carrig Cove,' she said. 'The lot of us traipsed over there the first week it came and the damn thing didn't show. It would be too embarrassing for all of us to go back over, and Ratty and Ned can't go on their own.'

'Why not?'

'You know why not. Two Ross kids on their own in Carrig Cove? They'll get slagged out of it, or worse. But if you went with them . . .'

'Me? I told you I haven't been back there since I was twelve.'

'Then it's about time you went,' she said. 'Or are you afraid to face your demons?'

'Demons? I've no demons,' I said, trying to hide my irritation.

'Don't raise your voice, Gorgeous. You'll wake the

natives.' Again she spoke lightly, teasing me; again her eyes were taking my measure. 'It's only a few hours out of your day. You'll get to know Ratty and Ned a bit better, they'll get their swim with the stupid fish. You never know, you might even enjoy reconnecting with your childhood haunts.'

We were at the split in the road. She kissed me and stepped back. 'Midday,' she said. 'Ned and Ratty will meet you at the church steps, three boys on a day trip. Don't forget your trunks, the little blue ones that look so good on you.' She tugged the belt on my black work trousers and smiled at me.

I opened my mouth to protest but I knew it was pointless. I was going to Carrig Cove tomorrow and I didn't seem to have any say in the matter. I couldn't help laughing even though I was annoyed. 'Tell Ned and Ratty to bring their bikes,' I said. 'I'm not driving. With the crowds going there these days there'll be nowhere to park.'

'Good thinking,' she said. 'I'll tell them. Goodnight, big guy.'

She winked and walked away from me, up the hill towards the big Victorian pile her family called home. She was barefoot and the skirt of her long dress swished about her legs as she moved. She knew I was watching her. I heard her laugh and she threw an exaggerated sway into her hips and twirled the flip-flops in her hand in salute, but she didn't turn her head. Not even slightly.

14
Gus

As we cycled over the causeway into Carrig Cove the next day I pulled a few yards ahead of Ned and Ratty. I needed some privacy as I returned to the old place. At first glance nothing had changed: grey row houses, the ugly fish factory, the gangly pier, the single pub, the grocer's shop, the butcher's shop, the Catholic church with its narrow steeple perched above the houses on High Street and square bell tower of the C of I church peeking through cedars up a lane to the left of Paudy's. All the same as that day six years ago when Ferdia and me left. Except everything was different. Cars lined the streets and there were tourists everywhere, window boxes stuffed with bright geraniums perched on every windowsill, even the low deep windowsills of the pub where I remembered old lads parking their behinds for their Sunday morning pints. Paudy's looked like it had recently acquired a fresh coat of paint, as did Monaghan's, and the telephone box on the corner sparkled cream and green in the sunlight.

I pulled over to the pavement and waited for the other two to catch up. Ned Cranny was a thickset tow-head, not renowned for his conversational skills; Ratty McRoth was a string bean. Ratty acted gormless but I knew he was sharp as a tack. We stowed our bikes in a corner of the car park behind the pub. When we walked out on the street I turned towards the beach but the lads called me back.

'Let's have a gander at the boats,' Ratty said.

'You're never thinking of going on one of the trips?' I said.

'Don't be daft,' Ned said. 'We want to see how it works, is all.'

'Well, from where I'm standing it looks as if you buy your tickets over in Monaghan's,' I said, flicking my chin at the signs directing people to the shop. 'Which doesn't surprise me. If there's a pound to be made Sly Monaghan will be having at least fifty pence of it, thank you very much.'

Ratty grinned and nodded and walked across to the pier anyway. Ned followed him. I shrugged. It was their day trip. What was it to me if they wanted to waste time gawking at trawlers?

The pier was crowded with families waiting for the next boat. Posters plastered along the wall described the tours as a 'FUN experience on GENUINE fishing trawlers! See the CARRIG COVE DOLPHIN or get your money back!'

The words 'RINN, THE CARRIG COVE DOLPHIN' were written in large red letters across a black-and-white photo of a leaping dolphin. It was as if the circus had come to town – *roll up, roll up, buy your tickets and ice-cream cones.*

'Bet that's just some dolphin picture they nicked from a book,' Ned said. 'Wonder why they call him Rinn?'

'No idea,' I said.

There were three trawlers tied up, one disembarking passengers and the other two taking them on, entire families including babies in pushchairs and grannies in hairnets. Everyone was chatting and laughing, clutching cameras and binoculars. Some of the women were dressed up for the day out, complete with Jackie Onassis sunglasses and headscarves to save their hairdos from the wind.

I recognised Dan Fogarty and his mate – John? Jack? Jim? – on the *Ella Louise*. He was telling people they had to stay seated at all times. I peered down and saw the nets had been removed and benches had been fitted anywhere the boat could take them. I pointed it out to Ned and Ratty.

'They're not normally there, then?' Ratty said.

'No,' I said. 'Fish don't need seats.'

'Ha ha,' Ned said, not really paying me any attention. 'Yeah, very funny.'

'Are you counting?' I asked. He was staring at the passengers on the trawler, moving his lips and bobbing his head as he glanced from one to the next. And Ratty was totting up the ones getting off the *Dulcie*. I frowned.

'Are we going swimming, or what?' I asked.

'In a bit,' Ned said. He pulled a notebook out of his pocket and wrote something down. Ratty glared at him, flicked his eyes at me, and Ned hurriedly shoved the notebook back into his trousers.

'What are you doing?' I said. 'What the blazes are you lads doing?'

'Nothing,' Ratty said. 'Just getting the lay of the land. People in Ross are curious about what's happening here, so we're sussing it out. No big deal.'

'By people you mean Maeve and Ali?' I said. I'd been had.

They looked at each other. 'Maybe,' Ned said.

'And I'm your – what? Cover? Guide? Chaperone? Well, it looks as though you can manage without me. No one will notice you in this mob. I'm off to the beach.'

'We'll follow you over when we're done here,' Ned said.

'Don't bother. I might just drown the pair of ye. I'm sure you can find your own way home,' I said. I was so furious it came out as a snarl. I turned and stormed up the pier, leaving Maeve's stooges to their information gathering.

The little beach, like the pier, was jammed. I found an empty spot near the water and changed into my togs. I ran into the waves and let the cold water stun me. I went under and swam out, out, as far as my breath would take me, away from the waders and splashers. I surfaced and looked around. The *Ella Louise* was pulling away from the pier, another boat was coming in. I could see two other trawlers far out in the bay looking like plastic boats in a bath, and the dolphin, tiny dolphin, leaping on cue. To the left, way in the distance, I could almost make out Ross and the yellow smudge of the Bay View Hotel.

What's going on? I thought. *Why did Maeve Grogan sleep with me last night? To get me to escort her two pet goons to Carrig Cove so they could figure out where all her daddy's business was going?*

I shook my head to get the water out of my eyes and ears. *Fuck you, Maeve Grogan,* I thought, and then gave a hollow laugh at my choice of expletives. To hell with her and Ali 'Snake-eyes' Matthews and their whole damn crowd. In another year school would be over. I'd be leaving Ross and heading to Dublin. From there the whole world beckoned. None of these people mattered to me, no one but Mam and Ferdia and, maybe, my old friend Dog.

I swam back to shore but my black mood was still with me, so when I saw a group of lads standing where I'd left my things, actually standing on them, I almost laughed aloud. They were watching me come out of the water, striking poses like they meant to give me hassle.

Oh yeah, I thought. *Try it. Just bloody try it.*

Conor McNessa, my old enemy, was right there in the middle of them.

Better and better.

I had to work hard to stop myself smiling as I let my hands clench into fists.

'What brings you here, McRoy?' Conor said as I approached. 'To what do we owe the, eh . . . pleasure?'

The other lads guffawed.

'Came to see what the fuss was about,' I said.

'You have to take a boat trip to see our Rinn,' a

guy with black hair said. The name Phelim Roche floated up from some dark place in my brain.

'Yeah,' JJ O'Toole said. 'You have to pay actual cash money to see the show.'

'I gathered,' I said. 'Figured I'd have a swim while I was here – that's still free.'

'Beaches no good in Ross?' Conor said, smiling that weasel smile of his. 'You had to come over here and slum it with us poor Carrig folk?'

'I'm Carrig Cove born and bred,' I said, 'and I'll swim where I damn well like. Now, if you boys get your tiny feet off my stuff, I'll be going.'

'Don't get your knickers in a twist,' JJ said. 'Oh, I forgot, you're not wearing them, ha ha ha.' He dragged his foot across my towel, opening it out and spreading my clothes across the grey sand. He ground his foot into my jeans, found the Y-fronts balled up inside and jumped away as if he'd been stung.

'Jaysus, McRoy,' Conor said. 'Did your mammy not teach you to change your undies at least once a month? Christ, the pong. You get that pong, lads?' He grabbed his nose with his left hand and fanned the air in front of his face with his right. The other boys followed suit, howling about the stink and tramping over my things as they clowned about. Conor stood back, watching them and smiling.

I put my head on one side and smiled back. 'I can sort your noses for you,' I said. 'Sort them so you'll smell nothing for a week.'

I stepped towards Conor, the one I most wanted to clock, the one I'd been wanting to clock since I was twelve years old. Phelim Roche immediately stopped clowning and stepped between us, like his nose was less important than Conor's. I raised my eyebrows.

'Still letting others take the heat for you, Conor?' I said. 'You always were all talk.'

Conor's grey eyes narrowed to slits. He motioned Phelim aside. 'You're not welcome here, McRoy,' he said. 'You're a Ross boy now – stay with your own.'

'Or what?' I said, stepping right up to him so my chest was almost touching his nose. I towered over him by at least five inches.

'Or we'll make you,' JJ said and he shoved himself between Conor and me, standing square on my Y-fronts as he did it.

I lost it then. I grabbed JJ by his T-shirt, lifted him off his feet and shoved him backwards into Conor. I leaned down as if to grab my stuff off the ground and, as I expected, JJ's foot shot up, making for my chin. I caught the incoming ankle and flipped JJ onto his arse. The rest of the lads fell back and I gave them a warning look before leaning down again to pick up my clothes.

'That was a yellow move, JJ,' a voice said. 'If you don't have the balls to fight fair, don't fight.'

I straightened up. 'Dog,' I said.

'Gus,' he said, and we moved towards each other, clapping each other on the shoulder in a half-embrace. 'What gives?' Dog said, frowning at Conor.

Conor shrugged. 'Nothing much. We were welcoming Gus back to Carrig Cove and he took it the wrong way.'

'Sure I did,' I said.

'Trouble with you, Gus,' Conor said, 'trouble with you is you don't have a sense of humour. Never did. Be seeing you, Dog.'

A couple of the lads hauled JJ O'Toole to his feet and they turned to leave, Phelim kicking one of my runners as he went. I moved after him but Dog stopped me.

'Let them go,' he said. 'They're not worth it.' He leaned down, picked up the runner and handed it to me. 'I can't believe you're here. It's been . . . how long?'

'Six years,' I said.

'Stone the crows,' Dog said. 'Too long. Come on, Gus, get your kit on. You're coming back to my place. Mam will kill me if she hears you were here and I didn't bring you home to see her.'

I shook my head, still pissed off about what had just

happened and still a little leery about whatever it was Ned and Ratty were up to. All in all, this visit had been a disaster and heading home seemed like a good idea.

'I should be going. Been told I'm not welcome, haven't I?' I said.

I jerked my head towards Conor and his gang. They'd reached the opening to the street. JJ turned around as they went through it and gave me the two fingers.

'Stay,' Dog said, 'If only to annoy the shite out of them.'

I laughed and considered. *Why not?* I thought. *This hassle with Conor McNessa wasn't my doing; why should I leave?*

'I came to swim with your dolphin,' I said, 'but it's otherwise occupied. Have you swum with it?'

He nodded. 'It was myself and a few others that swam with him first,' he said. He put his head on one side, like he was weighing something up. 'Can you stick around?' he said. 'Stay over? You can sleep at my place.'

Hannibal at the hotel had phoned this morning to tell me not to bother coming into work so I had nothing to do with my evening. *Damn it,* I thought. *I came here on a fool's errand, I may as well make something of it.*

'Why not?' I said, pulling my jeans up around my hips. 'But let's get off this beach. I'm getting burnt to a flippin' crisp.'

15
Gus

The kitchen was cool and fragrant. Bunches of dried flowers hung from the ceiling and the kitchen shelves were lined with labelled jars. Deirdre Cullen didn't recognise me immediately, but when Dog said my name she threw her arms around me and exclaimed over my height and how handsome I'd grown. I blushed and she laughed.

Deirdre was the prettiest mammy in Carrig Cove, though she was probably only five years younger than my own mam. Through the window I could see the garden where Dee grew the herbs she used to make the salves and ointments which had earned her the nickname The Witch on The Hill amongst the locals. She may have been the subject of gossip and derision in Carrig Cove but Deirdre had been warm and welcoming to Dog's friends, and going to her house for tea had always been a huge treat.

I sat at the big wooden table now and watched her potter around her kitchen, bare feet on grey flagstones, her dark hair flowing down her back and a long sleeveless dress clinging to her rather lovely body. She caught me staring and her lips twitched in amusement.

'I hear they're talking about bringing in water rationing and hosepipe bans soon,' I said. 'My mam is fretting about her garden. What'll you do, Deirdre?'

'Most of my herbs are Mediterranean,' she said. 'They can stand a bit of drought, but I have a rain barrel set up – you could do that for your mam. It'll catch what comes off the roof in the next thunderstorm and she'll have it for when she needs it. And tell her it's OK to put the water from the dishes on her flowers, once it's cooled down.'

She laid food on the table for Dog and me, and when Kit Crosby appeared a place was set for him. There was ham, cheddar, sliced tomatoes, hard-boiled eggs and hunks of brown bread. The salad leaves were odd colours and shapes but tasted better than anything I ever got at home. Deirdre hung around for as long as it took her to eat a sandwich, then she set a large straw hat on her head and went out to work in her garden. While I'd been making small talk with his mother, Dog had been whispering with Kit, something which seemed to concern me. When Dee left I turned to them and said, 'So?'

'So.' Dog said. He looked at Kit, who nodded his assent. 'We have plans for tonight. Late tonight. We're not telling you what exactly, only that you'll like it.'

'And until then,' Kit said, 'I'm thinking we should put your height and general manliness to good use. You, my friend, are going into Paudy's to buy a flagon of cider which we are going to take up Delaney's field.' He rubbed his hands together, grinning. 'Paudy won't sell drink to any of us local lads, but he'll never recognise you and there's no way he'll think you're under eighteen.'

'I'm not,' I said. 'I turned eighteen in March.'

'So did Conor McNessa,' Dog said, 'but Paudy won't sell him drink. Conor brought his birth cert in and showed it to him but Paudy said he wouldn't sell him anything, out of respect to Mrs McNessa. Conor was bulling.'

'What are we waiting for?' I said, standing up. 'Let's go.'

16

Emer

The shop had been manic the whole day. The thermometer hit twenty-nine at noon and showed no sign of dropping as the day crawled towards closing time. I tried to stop watching the clock because it seemed to have entered some time warp where every minute lasted an hour. All I could think of was midnight, midnight, midnight, the beach, the sea, the beach.

This was the pattern ever since the boat trips had begun three weeks before; long sweltering days slaving in the shop, dreaming of midnight when the beach belonged just to us, to Rinn and Fee and Kit and Dog and me.

Mam had to give a hand in the shop most days because it was so jammers with people, especially now we were selling the boat-trip tickets. You'd think Da would have been in great humour with so much extra trade but it had just given him one more thing to be cranky about.

He insisted on dealing with the boat tickets himself, saying they were too complicated for Mam and me. If the tickets were complicated that's because he set them up to be. He was determined that since the whole thing was his idea he should profit from it, and he convinced the boatmen the only way to make sure everyone got their share of customers was to sell the tickets centrally. He was running between the shop and the pier all day long, checking things were running smoothly and sorting out the 'wrinkles' in his system. I'd seen Dan and the others rolling their eyes behind his back more than once.

The clock hit five at last and the shop went quiet. Da took off his apron and headed to the door. 'Mind the place,' he said, as if Mam and myself hadn't the cop on to do it without being told.

I was down the back of the shop sweeping up a burst bag of sugar. As soon as I heard the door close I lay down on the floor. The tiles were cool against my skin. I closed my eyes.

Midnight, I thought. *Midnight.*

The bell above the door jangled. I sighed, rolled

onto one hip, opened my eyes and peeked between the display shelves and the stacks of boxes. Thickset ankles in heavy brown nylons crossed the shop towards the counter.

'Maura,' said Mrs Ryan's voice. 'You're in here a lot these days. It's like old times. Before your mishap.' I caught the inflection. Obviously Mrs Ryan, like Da, had little patience for back pain.

'All hands on deck,' Mam said. 'The ice-cream machine is in big demand this weather – I can manage that. It leaves Syl and Emer free to do everything else that needs doing.'

'Where is Emer?' Mrs Ryan said. I could hear her voice turning and presumed she was scanning the aisles, looking for me.

'Around here somewhere,' Mam said. 'What can I get you, Rita?'

'Twenty Benson and Hedges, please,' Mrs Ryan said. 'Emer's getting very pretty. Not that I'd say that in front of her – can't be filling girls' heads with notions. But she is. Very pretty. Has she a boyfriend?'

'Not that I know of,' Mam said.

'You should ask her straight out. I would.'

'I'd rather she tell me of her own accord,' Mam said. Her voice was firm. I could almost hear Mrs Ryan's eyebrows shoot upwards.

'Well,' Mrs Ryan said. 'I'd not have my Mary keeping secrets from me. You never know where that might lead.'

Mam didn't reply. I heard the till open and coins rattle.

'Your change, Rita,' Mam said.

'I've heard,' said Mrs Ryan, her voice lowering, 'I've heard there's kids swimming at night. With the dolphin. Down at the beach. Patsy Roche said he heard them at it when he was coming in on the boat late one night last week. Skinny-dipping, they were, Patsy said.'

I froze.

'He *heard* them skinny-dipping?' Mam said. 'Those are some ears Patsy has.'

I had to stick my fingers in my mouth to stifle a laugh. I curled up on the tiles with my arms wrapped about me. I wished I could see Mrs Ryan's face, though I could imagine it well enough. She'd be frowning, her eyes glaring black currants in her doughy cheeks. Her lips would be open, wobbling in outrage as she tried to form an adequate response.

'It's home in their beds they should have been at that time of night, like normal Christians,' she said.

'This hot weather's been shaking us up,' Mam said. 'And sure, don't we need shaking up every now and then or we get set in our ways.'

'There's nothing wrong with our ways,' Mrs Ryan snapped. 'All I can say is I'm glad it's not my Mary. And it isn't. I've checked her room every night since Patsy told me, and Mary's been where she should be – in bed asleep.'

'There you are then,' Mam said. The drawer of the till slammed closed. 'All's right with the world. Do you need anything else, Rita? It's closing time.'

Under the shelves I saw her walk Mrs Ryan across the floor, watched the door open and shut, heard the key turn in its lock. Mam's feet crossed back over to the counter and I heard the ice-cream machine whirring. Mam was cleaning it, my job usually.

She thinks I'm in the storeroom. I'll stand up in a minute, act as if I've just come back out, I thought, closing my eyes again. *Dog. Rinn. Our midnight beach.*

'Here,' Mam said.

I opened my eyes. Mam was looking down at me. She had two monster ninety-nines in her hands. She held one out to me as she took a huge bite out of the other. I sat up and took mine from her outstretched hand. She slid down onto the floor beside me. We both leaned against the fridge.

'This is probably the coolest spot in the county right now,' Mam said, her legs stuck out in front of her like mine. 'Better eat these fast before your da comes back and catches us.'

She began to laugh. I began to laugh. We stuffed ourselves, tears rolling down our cheeks at the thought of Da's face if he found us sitting on the floor of his shop, eating his ice cream, and three chocolate flakes sticking out of each cone.

17
Gus

By midnight we were bolloxed on cheap cider and half a bottle of cooking sherry Kit had pilfered from his ma's kitchen. We lay flat on the grass in Delaney's field, watching stars spin above our heads.

'C'mon, we'll be late,' Kit said, struggling to his feet. 'C'mon.'

'Where we going?' I said.

'S'prise,' Dog said. 'I told you if you stayed, there'd be a s'prise.' He got to his feet too quickly and lurched off to starboard a bit before steadying himself. 'C'mon,' he said, and grabbed my hand. I let him pull me to my feet though he was only two-thirds my size.

'Lez go,' Kit said. 'We're late. They'll be mad.'

'Who?' I said, 'What? Where?' I laughed as I watched both of them weaving down the hill in front of me. Being bigger has advantages – I was drunk for sure but not as langers as Dog and Kit.

At the bottom of Hill Street they stopped and shushed me.

'I'm not saying anything, yez head-the-balls,' I said. 'It's you two making the racket.'

'Ssssh!' Kit looked up and down the pavement with exaggerated care. 'All clear. C'mon.' He stepped out onto the road, beckoning us after him toward the beach.

'Couldn't have my old friend Gus coming all the way over here, first time in years, an' miss out on swimming with our dolphin. Not when you came over specially,' Dog said, turning and belting me one on the chest. 'But it's a secret. You have to promise not to tell.'

'Promise?' Kit said. 'Swear?'

'I swear,' I said, not entirely sure what I was swearing to.

'Right. You're in,' Dog said.

The strand seemed empty when we walked onto it but I saw Kit looking around as if he expected someone to be here, presumably whoever it was that'd be mad with us for being late. *Please,* I thought. *Don't let it be Conor or any of his mangy gang of gobshites*, but the two shadows that detached from the rocks to the right of us were girls. I recognised them from school. The redhead was Fedelma something-or-other. I didn't know the brunette's name. They both stared at me and then looked at Kit and Dog.

'What's he doing here?' the Fedelma girl said, obviously put out.

'You remember Gus McRoy?' Kit said. 'Gus'd like to swim with Rinn, is all.' He leaned in to kiss her and she drew back like he'd breathed fire in her face.

'You're pissed,' she said. 'You're fecking stocious.'

The other girl was watching Dog. She was one of those girls who looks ordinary from a distance, which is the only way I'd ever seen her before. Up close I could see that she was lovely: soft brown eyes, full lips, gorgeous skin.

'I'm Emer,' she said, turning to me. 'We swim every night, the four of us. We didn't expect . . . no one said . . . You're welcome, of course.'

Her eyes flicked back to Dog. I could see she was trying to gauge how drunk he was. Dog and Kit were shedding their clothes, flinging them off to right and left. Kit got one leg stuck in his jeans and toppled over onto the sand, giggling like a little kid. Dog began to laugh too and the pair of them became hysterical.

'You daft fecker,' Dog said. 'Can't hold your apple juice.' But from where I stood he was as drunk as

Kit, if not more so. His eyes were glazed and he was swaying. None of this was lost on the two girls.

'You're not seriously getting in the sea in that state?' Fedelma said.

'We're grand,' Kit said. 'Nothing a good belt of cold water won't fix. C'mon, get ready.'

She shook her head. 'I'm not going into the sea in the middle of the night with three half-cut morons,' she said. 'I have more sense and so does Emer.'

'Aw, c'mon,' Kit said. 'Don't be a spoilsport, Fee.' He made to grab her hand but she shook him off.

'Do what you like,' she said. 'Count me out.'

'Couldn't we just sit for a while?' Emer said to Dog. 'Don't you think—'

'I promised Gus we'd take him swimming with Rinn,' he said, turning away from her.

I saw her lay a hand on his arm and he brushed it aside roughly. 'Let's go, lads,' he said, and he headed towards the waves. Kit shrugged apologetically at Fedelma who gave him a filthy look, turned on her heel and stalked up the beach. Emer hesitated and looked at me.

'They're really drunk,' she said, her eyes full of concern. 'You all are. You shouldn't be swimming.'

'It's OK,' I said. 'I'm not as bad as they are and I'm sobering up fast. I won't let anything happen to them.'

She nodded. 'Thanks,' she said. She watched Dog run into the sea, then followed her friend away into the dark.

18
Gus

Dog and me must have woken his ma when we got back that night. No one could have slept through the racket we made getting into the house. My mam would have been up immediately, fussing over the state of us, but Dee Cullen left us to it. I collided with a chair and Dog tripped over his own feet as we made our way to his room in the dark. He insisted I take the bed and he dossed down on the floor. Around three o'clock I was half aware of him staggering to the bathroom and he was there a while. I must have slept through him coming back because he was on the floor again when I woke, his head under the sheet.

'Dog,' I said, leaning over the side of the bed. 'I'd better get going. Mam will be wondering where

I am. If I don't appear for breakfast she'll have me dead in a ditch.'

He groaned and turned to look up at me.

'Jaysus, man,' I said. 'You're grey in the face.'

'I feel like a piece of shite,' he said.

'D'you want a glass of water?'

'I'd kill for one,' he said.

I pulled on my clothes and went out to the kitchen. When I came back Dog had managed to haul himself off the carpet and was sitting on the edge of the bed holding his head in his hands. He took the glass from me and began to gulp the water down.

'Easy, man,' I said. 'Take a breather. Make sure it's going to stay put.'

He took the glass away from his face. 'So, what did you think of our Rinn?' he said.

'Well,' I said. 'It was an experience I won't forget in a hurry.'

Dog grimaced. 'Dunno what got into him. He wouldn't have been that rough if the girls were in the water. He's always a bit more lively around us lads but that was a bit much.'

I laughed. 'I'm not saying it wasn't fun. It was. But there were a few times I thought one of us would get hit. We three weren't in the best state for quick reactions.'

'We got away with it,' Dog said.

'We did,' I said. 'With Rinn anyway. Not sure yourself and Kit are in your girlfriends' best books, though.'

Dog shrugged like he didn't care but his face told a different story.

'An apology might do the trick,' I said.

He lay down on the bed. 'I'll think about it later,' he said. 'Right now I need some more kip.'

'You know it's Saturday, right? Don't you have hurley practice?'

'I can miss it for once. You'll find your own way out?'

'I think I can manage that,' I said. 'Last night was a blast, though you look like you might be regretting it.'

'Hey, no regrets, man,' Dog said, smiling weakily. 'Never.'

He held up a hand and I slapped mine against it before heading to the door. 'Tell Deirdre I said goodbye,' I said.

He grunted his assent and flopped back onto the pillows.

As I cycled across the causeway I wondered if I should have told Dog about Ned Cranny and Ratty McRoth poking around the boats the day before, taking notes for Maeve Grogan. I knew I should but I didn't like admitting I'd been duped. The thing is, at that moment, I couldn't see the point of what they'd been doing so I couldn't see any harm in it either. I had no idea – none – what Maeve was planning, and no notion at all of how mad things would get.

19

Emer

It was barely gone nine. Da had only just turned the key in the shop door and flipped the sign to open. I was down the back pushing the fresh milk to the furthest reaches of the fridge and pulling yesterday's leftovers to the front when I heard the bell jangle. I knew it was Dog who'd come in, knew without turning my head.

He's come to make up with me, I thought. *Well, I'll not make it easy for him.*

Last night I'd been worried sick about him. I'd lain awake for hours, fretting, wondering if he and Kit and Gus McRoy had made it home in one piece. This morning I was angry. I couldn't believe the way he'd spoken to me, the way he'd shoved my hand off him.

He'd been drunk, I knew, but what if that surly boy was the real Dog Cullen? I'd seen another side of him and I didn't like it very much.

I could feel his eyes on me but I kept on rearranging the milk bottles and didn't turn around.

'Do you want something?' I heard Da say.

Dog mumbled a few words, so low they could have been anything.

'What did you say?' Da snarled. 'Speak up, for heaven's sake. Why can't young people these days speak properly?'

'A pint of milk,' Dog said. 'Please.'

'That'll be in the fridge, where it always is. Emer, give this young lad a bottle of milk.'

I grabbed a bottle by the neck and walked up the shop. Dog met me halfway and I held the milk towards him. He reached out to take it and tried to make me look at him but I wouldn't. I let go the bottle and turned away, leaving him standing there. I walked to the back of the shop, went through to the storeroom and shut the door firmly behind me. I didn't go back out till I heard the bell ding again and knew he was gone.

'What was that?' Da said. 'Is something going on between you and that young Cullen fella?'

I shook my head.

Da's eyes narrowed to slits. 'There'd better not be,' he said. 'His mother's stone mad and I hear his da was a tinker. There's barely a drop of religion of any persuasion to be had between the two of them. As far as I can see that young fella was brought up practically heathen.'

He slammed the register shut and rolled his eyes as Fee came through the door.

'You,' he said to her. 'Get your chatter over sharpish. Half the village will be in in a minute, all wanting to be served at once.' He glared at me. 'I've things to do in the storeroom,' he said. 'Sort the newspapers.'

When Da was gone Fee said, 'I saw Dog leaving. What did he say? Did he apologise?'

'I didn't give him the chance,' I said.

'Good for you,' Fee said. 'What the hell made them think it was OK to bring that Gus McRoy fella anyway? And without telling us?'

I nodded, though I couldn't care less about that. It was the way Dog had looked at me, the way he'd pushed my hand away that upset me. It was him being so stupidly reckless with his own life that had me angry.

'He looked like death warmed up. I'd say he has a head on him this morning,' Fee said. 'Serves him right. At least Dog got out of bed to try and make it up with you. No sign of Kit. I hope he's dying, I really do.'

I nodded again.

'So,' Fee said. 'Do we go to the beach tonight? Just turn up, like nothing's happened? Or make them stew a little longer?'

'You can,' I said, 'but I won't. I didn't sleep much last night.'

'Oh,' she said. 'OK. I won't go if you don't. But I'll see you later on, after the shop closes?'

I shook my head. 'I'm all in,' I said. 'I want some time to think. D'you mind?'

'No,' she said, though I could tell she did. 'I'd better go before your da comes back and chews me out of it.'

I nodded.

'But you'll go swimming again, Emer?' she said. 'It's not finished between you and Dog?'

I shrugged. I felt tears welling in my eyes and I blinked furiously.

'Ah, Emer,' she said, her pique gone in an instant. 'He's a boy. They can't stand to lose face in front of each other. If they have to choose between pissing off their girlfriend and looking bad in front of another fella, their pride will win every time.'

‘I know,’ I said. ‘But I have pride too.’

‘Of course you do,’ she said. ‘But you’ll let him apologise if he tries again?’

I nodded and she gave me a quick hug.

‘You still here, Fedelma Hennessy?’ Da’s voice came from the corridor.

‘No, Mr Monaghan,’ Fee shouted. ‘I left five minutes ago. It’s just my echo you’re hearing, hearing, hearing.’

She grinned at me and ran for the door. Rory was outside waiting for her. He waved in at me and I waved back. I put the last stack of newspapers up on the shelves and began to gather up the string that had bound them, running each length around my fingers and securing it with a tight little knot.

20
Emer

What I said to Fee was true – I was wrecked. Still I woke automatically at ten minutes to midnight just like I'd been waking every night for the past month.

Go back to sleep, I told myself. But my body was awake, ready to go, anticipating the balmy night air and fresh cold water. And kisses and exploring fingers. Lips on my skin and whispers tangling in my hair.

For the last few weeks our midnight swims were what I lived for, the secret I held tight to me all day. Every night I was in bed by ten so I could catch a couple of hours' nap before sneaking out onto the street and crossing to the beach where the others were waiting, waiting to call Rinn to us. Every night we swam for as long as Rinn stayed around. Afterwards we lay on the beach together, me in Dog's arms and

Fee in Kit's. Recently Fee and Kit had taken to going a little further up the beach, ducking behind a small crop of rocks for privacy. I didn't know how far Fee was letting Kit go, but I figured it was further than just kissing. Maybe they were going all the way, making love, having sex.

Sex. It seemed like such a big step to take, like an end to everything I'd known till now – childhood, family ties, doing what was expected of me – and a beginning of all I didn't know and wasn't sure I was ready for. I was only letting Dog kiss me and touch me outside my swimsuit. I knew he was getting frustrated. So was I. I wanted him. Wanted him so much I thought I'd explode. But I was scared. I'd thought love and sex were somewhere off in my future, something that would happen in a few years, after school had ended and college had begun, ever supposing Mam persuaded Da to let me go. Da was always saying there was no point sending girls to college, that I'd only go and get married as soon as I qualified and waste the lot of it. But Mam wanted me to go and she swore she'd get Da to agree. I figured if I did what Da wanted for another year, my life would be my own once I finished school.

I hadn't expected love to turn up this summer. I hadn't bargained for a dolphin in the bay, for endless sunshine, more sun than any of us had ever seen before; brown skin, more skin than any of us had ever seen before.

And night swimming. I hadn't bargained on night swimming. I'd never imagined myself climbing out my window at midnight, lying in a boy's arms on the sand in the dark. These last few weeks I hadn't given a thought to next year or any year other than this year, this summer, this moment, right now. Lying in bed that night I realised I'd stopped daydreaming about going to college because going to college would mean separation from Dog.

Are you really going to trade in your big plans for some boy, Emer Monaghan? Is that who you are now?

Well, it didn't matter if it was, because it was most likely over. Fee was right. Dog was proud. He'd come to apologise this morning and I hadn't let him. He wouldn't come again. Dog and I were through. But that didn't mean I had to give up Rinn too. I looked at my watch. It was one o'clock. If Dog and Kit had gone swimming they should have gone home by now. I rolled upright, grabbed my towel and slipped through the window into the yard.

When I got to the beach I looked around to make sure I had the place to myself. The moon was bright; I didn't have to wait for my eyes to adjust to the darkness. I shed my clothes and walked into the sea.

Rinn was there already, waiting. He whistled his usual greeting and then he was quiet, as he always was with me. We swam together and when I stopped, he stopped and let me come close, close enough to touch him.

I knew I shouldn't, knew it was a daft thing to do. If he reacted badly, lashed out, I was alone, there was no one to help me. But I knew, thought I knew, it would be all right, so I reached out. For a heart-stopping moment I ran my fingers gently over his nose, his face and, Rinn and me, we held each other's eye. He made a low buzzing sound, like a cat's rumbling purr. I felt it vibrate through my fingers and up my arm. Then he turned, dived, and was gone.

I waded back to the shore with that touch singing on my palm. A fierce joy surged through me. I felt as if I had spoken to the ocean itself and in response, it had called my name.

21
Emer

Fee left me alone till Monday, when she and Rory appeared on the dot of twelve-thirty.

'Taking Emer outside for her lunch break, Mr M,' she said, waving a tinfoil package in the air. 'And don't worry, these sandwiches are made entirely from cheese slices and tomatoes purchased here in this very shop.' She grabbed my arm and hustled me out the door, with Da yelling, 'Thirty minutes, no more,' after us.

'Jaysus, your da's a slave driver,' she said. 'Does he still not pay you a bean?'

I shook my head. 'He says the shop will be mine one day and sure doesn't he feed and clothe me. It'll be worth it if he lets me go to college next year.'

'He still hasn't said yes?'

'Not yet.'

'What if' – Fee frowned – 'what if he gets so used to you working in the shop he decides he can't do without you?'

The horror must have shown plainly on my face because she told Rory to go read his book on the pier and pushed me over to the bench beside the phone box. She sat me down and shoved a sandwich into my hand.

'Emer, you know you're duty-bound to rebel?' she said. 'You do understand that's part of the job description of being a teenager, right?'

I sat there like a lump, staring at her.

'Being good will get you nowhere with your da,' she said. 'You could start being less flippin' efficient, don't be anticipating what needs doing. In fact, wait until you've been asked to do it ten times.'

'I never thought . . .' So many horrible ideas were crashing through my brain at once and I couldn't get them into words.

'You never thought that maybe your da intends you to be his slave forever? You really are a bit of a noodle, Emer. For an intelligent girl, I mean. Eat up.' She raised my hand to my face and pushed the sandwich towards my open mouth.

'So,' she said. 'Are we going swimming tonight or what?'

'My question exactly.' Kit appeared from the other side of the phone box. He was alone. 'Are me and Dog forgiven for the other night or do we have to do some elaborate and fiendish penance of your devising?'

Fee regarded him with a raised eyebrow. 'You'd like that, wouldn't you?' she said, a smile twitching at her lip. 'We'll see what we can think up, won't we Emer?'

I pulled a face at the two of them, still too haunted by the idea of being stuck in the shop for the rest of my natural life to join in the banter.

'Seriously but,' Kit said. 'Will you two be coming tonight or what? It's not that *I* mind so much, but Dog's been a total misery guts since Friday. I was all up for going without you two on Saturday night, but he wouldn't do it. Said there was no point.'

Fee punched him on the arm. 'You'd have gone without us?' she said. 'You're not very good at this boyfriend thing, are you?'

'There's never been any complaints before,' he said, which earned him another thump.

'You want evidence of my affection?' he said, jumping to his feet and strolling into the middle of the road.

'You're all right,' Fee said, laughing. 'Don't break sweat on my account.'

'Oh, but I will,' Kit said. He stayed where he was, even though there was a car coming down the road. It honked its horn and drove around him. 'I will announce my love to the entire village, if that's what you want.' He turned around and spread his arms. 'GOOD FOLK OF CARRIG COVE,' he shouted. 'I WISH TO ANNOUNCE MY UNDYING L—'

'Shut up, you big eejit,' Fee hissed, running out onto the road and grabbing him. She pulled him back towards the bench. Kit pretended to struggle and opened his mouth as if to start shouting again and Fee clamped a hand across his face.

'Will you stop clowning?' she said. 'The whole place is watching.'

'Who?' he mumbled through her fingers. 'Who's watching?'

'All of them,' she said. 'Village of the squinting feckin' windows, this is. The lace curtains are always twitching.'

'Let's give them something to watch, then,' Kit said and he grabbed Fee around the waist and began kissing her neck.

She giggled and pushed him away. 'Give over,' she said. 'My ma will have heard about this before I get home, if she hasn't heard already. Am I right, Emer?'

'Leave me out of it,' I said. 'You two are putting me clean off my lunch.'

Fee was right. Other people had heard, other people had seen. Da had a face on him like thunder when I got back in the shop.

'What was that?' he said. 'Making a show of yourselves out on the street, in front of everybody. You're not involved with that young layabout, Kit Crosby?'

'He's a friend,' I said.

'What sort of friend?'

'A friend friend.'

'Don't cheek me, Miss. I'll not have a daughter of mine shouting and roaring and acting the tart for the whole world to see.'

'Acting the tart?' I spluttered, shocked at this sudden attack. I wasn't about to announce to my da that Fee was the one going with Kit. He'd only tell her mam and Fee's mam was as strict with Fee as Da was with me.

'What do you think people are saying about you, hanging around the street with half nothing on? Walking around the village in those shorts? You look like a whore.'

Whore. My da just called me a whore.

I opened my mouth to say something but I

couldn't speak, I couldn't think. I just stood there staring at him, blinking, trying not to cry.

'Sylvester!' Mam appeared from the kitchen. She marched over to the shop door, closed it quietly, turned the key in the lock and flipped the sign. Her face was white when she turned back to Da but she said nothing and this seemed to fluster Da more than if she'd laid into him straight off.

'We have a reputation to uphold in this village,' he began. 'I won't have people calling her names—'

'The only one I hear calling our daughter names is you,' Mam said. Then, over her shoulder to me, 'Leave us, Emer. There's a good girl.'

I went into my room, sat on the bed and hugged my knees tight to my chin. I could hear Da's voice rising and falling. I caught the gist of it – *I wasn't a little girl any more . . . They needed to watch me or I'd get myself in trouble . . . That young tearaway Dog Cullen was making goo-goo eyes at me.*

I don't know what Mam said in reply – she was speaking too low for me to make out her words. It went quiet after a bit. They must have unlocked the shop door because I heard the bell going and the murmur of voices. I lay back on my bed and let myself drift away, dreaming of the sea as the shop bell ding-dinged in the distance.

22
Gus

Mam had been droning on about Ferdia the entire day. He hadn't written her for two weeks. *Was he homesick? Was he dead?* I tried to calm Mam down, reminded her that Ferdia wasn't the best for writing, but that only set her off on how unappreciated she felt. *Wasn't she paying his bed and board in Dublin so he could spend the summer training in a sport she couldn't abide in the first place? What mother wants her son spending his days being knocked about, having his lovely face punched, his nose broken and God knows what damage to his head? Did he not realise the sacrifices she was making? Did he never think of her at all?*

She was like a clockwork toy, winding herself up and running herself down, clacking around the rooms, complaining as she went. If I could have gotten my hands on my baby brother, I'd have cheerfully murdered him. Eleven p.m. and she was still at it. I had to get out of the house. I walked down the town to clear my head. It was no accident that I went towards the harbour and the Bay View Hotel. If Maeve was out and about at this hour, that's where she'd be. If I saw her I'd give her a piece of my mind for sending me over to Carrig Cove with her spies. At least that's what I told myself I'd do. Every time I closed my eyes I could see her body, feel her skin under my hands. I knew she only had to crook her little finger and I'd coming running.

A few yards short of the harbour I stopped at a corner to light a cigarette. That's when I heard voices, five or six voices. Maeve's, Ali's, Ned Cranny's, Ratty McRoth's, another girl, another boy. I couldn't see anyone but I could tell by the way their voices were being amplified that they were within the harbour walls, among the boats. I was about to saunter over to the pier, look down and say, 'How's it going? What gives?', just to see what they did, but I heard Ali Matthews's voice say, 'Shhhh, keep it quiet, will you?' and Maeve's voice saying, 'Hurry up, get in. We haven't got all night,' so I stopped, stayed in the shadows.

I tried to piece together what I was hearing: *Steady*

the boat . . . mind the fish . . . Carrig Cove . . . Whisht, will you? . . . Switch off the motor, row in . . . give it the fish, one at a time . . . We'll be waiting . . . we'll be ready when you get back.

No? NO!

That would be insane. They couldn't actually think such a mad idea would work? I should forget it, go home to my bed. But I didn't. I couldn't risk it. They'd involved me by sending me over to Carrig with Ratty and Ned. I'd helped them plan this, without meaning to. I had to do something to stop them. I ran back to the house, got my bike out of the shed and rode over to Carrig Cove like a pack of wolves were snapping at my arse.

23
Emer

I slept for hours. When I woke my watch said eleven-thirty. I'd missed dinner but there was time enough to grab something from the fridge to take with me to the beach.

I nearly jumped out of my skin when I flicked the kitchen light on and Mam was there, sitting at the table. She turned her head, gave me a small smile and indicated the covered plate beside her. I sat down and lifted the cover off to see a salad – corned beef, tomato, potato salad, coleslaw, lettuce.

'I knew you'd be hungry,' Mam said. There were tears on her cheeks. A balled hanky sat on the table.

'Mam,' I said.

'Eat,' she said. 'There's time.'

I stared at her.

'Eat,' she said.

I began shovelling food into my mouth, wondering what to say. *What did she know? How did she know?*

'You need to be careful not to rile your father, Emer,' she said. 'Just for this one last year till you turn eighteen. One more year and you can leave this place. Don't let anyone stop you.'

I put down my fork. 'Fee says Da thinks he can make me stay here working in the shop,' I said. 'Does he?'

Mam nodded. She stared at the window though it was a big black mirror now the kitchen light was on.

'Your father expects you to take over the shop when he retires,' she said, 'like he was expected to take it over from his parents. He wanted to do accountancy, you know. His father wouldn't have it. Said there was a livelihood being handed him on a platter and he'd damn well like or lump it. Your father didn't get to go to college and he can't see the point in you going. I just about had him convinced you should get a qualification and teach until he's older, but now with the shop so busy . . . I'll talk him around. This thing with the dolphin will die down. It'll leave, or people will get bored with it. When it's not so hectic he'll see sense. I'll make him.'

She turned to face me. 'You're in love, aren't you?'

I felt tears forming. I nodded.

She reached forwards and took my chin in one hand. 'I can't tell you what to do, sweetheart,' she said. 'Just remember what you want in life. Don't let any man take your dreams away from you.'

'But Dog isn't—'

'Your dad was young and almost handsome once,' she said. 'He's right, you know, him and Rita Ryan. About my bad back. There's nothing wrong with it, never was.'

I frowned. Waited.

'When you were little you were my excuse for staying out of the shop but once you turned ten your Dad insisted he needed me to work. I thought I'd go insane, around him every day, hour in, hour out. I came close to a breakdown. I told Dr Scanlon I was going to leave, take you and leave. Dr Scanlon told me not to, said we'd find another way. He told your Dad I'd injured my back. Sometimes I wish I'd had the strength to tell the truth and leave, but I gave in and went along with the lie.'

I didn't know what to say. I'd sometimes wondered how Mam wound up with Da. I couldn't imagine them falling in love but I couldn't imagine them apart either.

She patted my cheek and stood up from the table. 'Be careful. OK?'

I nodded.

'I'll go to bed. Turn off the lights before you leave,' she said as she went to the door. 'Goodnight, love.'

'Goodnight, Mam,' I said.

I finished the salad, wiped the plate clean and tiptoed back to my room. I stood for a moment at the window. It was too late, too late to be careful. I loved Dog and nothing else mattered to me now. I pushed the sash up and slipped out into the night.

24
Emer

Dog was waiting at the side gate. He put a finger to my lips to warn me off speaking and pointed upwards. Every first-floor window on the street was open, the sleeping houses trying to suck in whatever cool air the night had to offer. He took my hand and we walked in silence, picking up Fee and Kit at the Hill Street turn. We tiptoed across the road together and walked onto the beach.

'There's someone here,' Fee whispered, squinting into the shadows.

'It's me,' a voice said. Gus McRoy came forward from the rocks, wheeling a bicycle with one hand. He must have arrived just before us; he was out of breath.

'Gus,' Dog said, glancing at me and Fee. 'What gives?'

‘I had to come,’ Gus said. ‘I didn’t know, I swear. I had no idea what they were planning. I came as soon as I realised.’

‘Realised what?’ Kit said. ‘What are you talking about?’

Gus took a deep breath and wiped his free hand across his mouth. ‘They’ve taken your dolphin,’ he said.

‘What?’ Dog began to laugh. We all did. ‘Don’t be daft. You can’t “take” a dolphin.’ His laugh faltered as Gus shook his head vehemently.

‘You can. They have. It’s an insane plan, but it’s working. Ali Matthews, Ned Cranny and Ratty McRoth came over here with a skiff full of fish and right now they’re heading across the bay with Rinn following behind them. I saw the boat turn back for Ross as I crossed the causeway, saw them tossing fish for Rinn, saw him swimming after the boat.’

We stared at him like he had ten heads.

‘I was out for a walk,’ he said, sounding the words out slowly and deliberately as if he was speaking a foreign language. ‘There was a bunch of kids down at the harbour, Maeve Grogan’s crowd, so I hid in the shadows to see what they were up to. They were loading a heavy bag onto a skiff and Maeve Grogan was giving directions and telling everyone to keep their voices down. I heard her tell them to lead "it" back, to bring "it" as far into the harbour as they could. That was when the penny dropped and I realised they were talking about Rinn.'

He stood there, waiting for us to take in what he'd said.

'They're. Kidnapping. Your. Dolphin,' he said, when none of us reacted.

'I don't understand,' Fee said. 'What'll they do when they get him to Ross? They can't actually trap Rinn in the harbour, so what's the point?'

Gus shook his head. 'I don't know what the rest of their daft plan is,' he said. 'I can only tell you what I overheard. I cycled here as fast as I could.'

'Don't you have a car?' Kit said. 'Why didn't you drive?'

Gus looked sheepish. 'They'd have heard me, seen my car on the causeway. It's yellow, hard to miss. They can't know I'm here. I have to live with them, Kit.'

Kit snorted but Dog nodded. 'Thanks for coming, Gus,' he said. 'Appreciate it.' He held out his hand for Gus to shake and I saw the older boy hesitate. Dog saw too. 'What?' he said.

'I ... I think I helped them,' Gus said. 'Inadvertently, I mean. When I was here on Friday last, I came over with those two – Ned Cranny and

Ratty McRoth. Maeve Grogan asked me to bring them over. She said they wanted to swim with Rinn but when they got here they only seemed interested in checking out the boat trips, so I left them to it. They were taking notes.'

'Taking notes?' Kit said. 'And you didn't suspect something?'

Gus spread his hands out in appeal. 'Who the hell would think this was what they were about? I thought Maeve was curious and just wanted to know what was going on here. Her father's hotel has been losing business since Rinn arrived. I never imagined . . . I would have said something if I'd thought . . .'

Dog nodded. 'You couldn't have known,' he said. He held his hand out again and this time Gus took it. 'Where was the skiff when you last saw it?' Dog asked.

'Passing Bishop's Rock,' Gus said. 'It has an outboard motor. They'll switch it on once they're far enough away not to be heard. I'd say they'll make Ross in thirty minutes.'

'Unless Rinn doesn't cooperate,' Fee said.

'That's right,' I said. 'He's not going to follow like a lamb, so it may take them longer than they expect.'

Dog was thinking. 'We need to—'

'Hang on,' Gus said. 'Don't say anything till I've gone.'

'We trust you, man,' Dog said.

'I know,' Gus said. 'But I'd rather there be no doubt. Good luck.' He mounted his bike and cycled away into the dark.

'OK,' Kit said, looking at Dog. 'What are we going to do?'

'We're going to wake Dan Fogarty,' Dog said. 'That's what we're going to do.'

25
Emer

Dan stood in the doorway, blinking at the four of us.

'Ring Jim, tell him I need him down at the boat immediately, if not sooner,' he said to his wife, Stella, who'd appeared behind him halfway through our story. She handed Dan a pair of trousers and a jumper, which he pulled on over his pyjamas. Stella took the receiver off the wall and began dialling as Dan grabbed the keys for the *Ella Louise* and shooed us out the front door ahead of him.

'You have a plan for when we get to Ross, Dog?' he said.

'A few ideas for a diversion. Kit and Fee are going to sort that. And then we do whatever the hell it takes to get Rinn back,' Dog said. 'That's my plan.'

Dan nodded. 'Right you are,' he said. 'But let's

organise ourselves a little more backup before we go. Let Kit sort the diversion, Fee. Martin, Patsy and Mickser McCabe, none of them have phones. I need you to go wake them, tell them the score. I'm certain they'll follow us over. Dog, Emer, you come on the *Ella Lou* with me.'

We'd the trawler ready to leave by the time Jim arrived and once he was on board we pushed off from the pier and began chugging into the bay. I could see Dog getting a focused look on his face, as if he was chasing our options through his mind. I left him alone.

'They've too big a head start to chase down, so we'll aim for the element of surprise instead. Try sneaking up on them,' Dan said. 'If we cut straight across the middle of the bay they'll see us for sure, so we'll stay close to the cliffs and circle the bay.'

'Won't they hear our engine?' I asked Dan.

'The noise from their own will drown ours,' he said.

He handed me a pair of binoculars. 'Scan the water for the skiff and let me know the second you spot it. And keep an eye out for Rinn. He may decide he's had enough and turn for home. No point fetching up in Ross ready for a showdown if the main player has already left the scene.'

I raised the glasses to my eyes. The moon was full so I could see quite a lot of the bay, but we were nearly at Ross when I spotted the skiff.

'There they are,' I said.

Everyone followed my pointing finger. The boat was barely moving over the water. I guessed Rinn wasn't making it easy for them.

'What do you reckon, Dan?' Jim said. 'Are we too far away to cut them off before they make the harbour?'

'I think we'd be taking a big chance,' Dan said. 'The other trawlers have radioed that they are on their way. We should wait. Play the long game. We need to figure out what exactly it is they're planning before we decide our next move. Right, Dog?'

'What? Right, right.' Dog was glaring into the distance after the skiff, as if he could sink it with a look. 'Rinn is definitely out there?'

I raised the glasses back to my face. 'I can see movements in the water. I think they just threw a fish at him.'

'Can you see Ross?'

'Only the streetlights,' I said, turning the glasses to shore. 'It's all shadows. Hold on. Did you see that? A light. Someone on the shore flashed a light.' I looked back at the boat. I could make out the figures on it now and I saw one turn and make a cutting gesture with his hand.

'Switch off the engine, Dan,' I hissed.

The *Ella Louise* fell silent and seconds later the other boat cut its motor. We heard the splash of oars hitting water. We heard a voice say, 'Let's get this animal into the harbour and close the trap on him.'

26

Gus

When I got back across the causeway I aimed straight for the church on the highest point of the town. I'd get the best view from there and there'd be no one about to see me. I stashed my bike inside the gate, went into the yard and climbed the church steps. Maeve had timed her raid well. The moon was full in a cloudless sky. I spotted the skiff easily. It was nearly back at Ross harbour.

I reckoned Dog and the others would enlist the help of one of the fishermen so I scanned the water for a trawler. When I looked over towards the cliffs I spotted one, a shadow within the shadows, not easily seen unless you were looking for it.

Dog was on the chase. I sat myself down on the top step to watch the show. Maeve's plan was audacious, I'd give her that. Who else would attempt to kidnap a wild dolphin? Who else would convince a heap of lads to try and make it happen? But when it came down to the wire I'd be rooting for Carrig Cove. I was furious with Maeve for using me, furious that I'd been made a fool of in front of my best friend and in front of the lads here in Ross.

Come on, Dog, I thought. *Show these arrogant arseholes they can't get away with this.*

The skiff cut its outboard motor and I saw the oars swing wildly out over the water.

Ned and Ratty will do all the grafting, I thought. *Ali will be the one giving orders, even though the boat belongs to Ned's da.*

I could see figures standing around on the harbour wall, their shapes clear in the orange light of the street lamps. It was easy to pick out Maeve – she was taller than the other girls. Someone flicked a torch on and off – answering flashes came from the skiff.

The one thing I couldn't fathom was how Maeve intended to trap Rinn. I concentrated on the pier, scrunching my eyes to force the details into focus. By the way they were standing, I realised a few of the figures were holding ropes.

The pontoons. Of course.

The Bay View kept two pontoons in the harbour,

floating docks for hotel guests to swim out to, something to sunbathe on when the shadows of the town fell inconveniently across the pier. You could always tell who the current favourites were in Maeve's inner circle by which kids got to hang out on the pontoons. Ross harbour was deep, deeper than Carrig Cove. The harbour wall was built in an L-shape, an arm crooked against the tide, protecting the boats moored within. Its opening was relatively small. If Maeve and her crew managed to lead Rinn inside, they could easily pull the pontoons across to form a barrier. Of course the dolphin could swim under the pontoons and escape, but if they'd rigged something to hang below the pontoons and block its exit – nets maybe – they might have a chance of holding him.

The skiff was almost at the harbour wall now. I stood up to get a better view but it dissolved into the shadows. I looked over at the fishing boat.

What was it waiting for? Why didn't Dog do something?

A slight mist was rising on the water, making it difficult to see the trawler. Was it even still there? I'd see better if I came down a few steps. I was about to move from the doorway of the church when I heard bicycle wheels, a heap of them, coming along the road from Carrig Cove. I shrank back against the door as the riders came to halt at the gates below me.

'Right, lads,' a voice said. 'We'll leave the bikes here. They'll be out of harm's way and ready for a quick getaway once we're done.'

Bollocks. Fucking Conor Mc-fucking-Nessa. Bollocks, bollocks, bollocks.

27
Gus

'Kit will give each of you what you need,' I heard Conor say. 'Then fan out across the town, like we discussed. Get in position and set them up, ready to go. Wait for the signal. Mind none of you start without Kit's signal.'

I saw heads nodding and heard whispered yeahs. I could see someone – I presumed it was Kit – taking things out of a rucksack and passing them around.

'Everyone got some?' he asked. 'And matches? You all have matches, right?'

Heads nodded. Someone held out a hand and Kit shoved something into it.

'Good. Off you go.' Conor's voice. 'You too, Kit. I'll stay up here with JJ and watch how things unfold.'

I saw Kit hesitate, but he left with the rest of the

lads. As soon as they were gone Conor and JJ lit up cigarettes.

'Do you think the fishermen will come, Conor?' JJ said.

'Of course they will,' Conor said. 'It's our flipping dolphin. We have to get it back.'

So that's why the trawler was staying out in the bay. She was waiting for the rest of the Carrig Cove posse to arrive. But they didn't know about the pontoons. I wished I could let them know. If it had been Kit at the bottom of the steps I'd have been down like a shot, to tell. Kit could have cycled back to Carrig, had someone radio the *Ella Louise*. But nothing would get me down the steps to tell Conor McNessa. Wild horses, wild fecking horses. No chance in hell.

It was already too late anyway. The figures down in the harbour began yelling and whooping. I could see movements, people pulling ropes. Rinn must have followed the skiff into the trap and now it was being closed on him.

'What the hell's going on down there?' Conor said. 'Jesus. Have they actually trapped Rinn? They have, the feckin' smart arses.'

'Feck! Feck! Now what?' JJ said. 'Are we too late? Are we too feckin' late?'

'The night's not over yet,' Conor said. 'Dog will think of something. He's the man, is Dog.'

I smiled in the shadows.

Yes, I thought. *Even an arrogant little shite like you knows Dog is the man. And you're right, Dog will think of something.*

And something was happening. Was that the purr of engines I could hear through the din the Ross kids were making?

Yes.

A light came on in the bay and the celebrations on the quayside stopped abruptly. A boat sat out in the water facing Ross. Maeve was the first to recover. I saw her body against the glare of the light. Her hands went to her hips, defiant.

'You're too late,' she yelled. 'We've got your precious fish. He's going to be our guest for a while. He'll soon figure out he chose the wrong town to hang out in when he chose your little dive.' She looked backwards into the harbour behind her, which I guessed was now shut in like a swimming pool. 'You'll love it here, Fish-pie. We know how to treat our guests. It'll be salmon all the way for you.'

She turned back to face the trawler, and stood there bold as brass, daring it to come and rescue the Carrig Cove money-spinner. But her moment of triumph was spoiled. A loud explosion split the air and she and everyone else on the pier instinctively ducked. There was another thunderous bang from somewhere over on Strand Road, and another from the bottom of Church Street, another from behind the hotel.

CRAACCCKK, CRRRAACK, ZZZWIIIPP, WWWHHHHAAAAP, FFFIIZZZKK.

The kids on the pier crouched, hands over their heads, spinning towards each successive noise in horror.

Jesus! I thought. *Explosives? Kit and the lads have set off explosives?*

It took me a moment to realise it was fireworks, not semtex. Bangers, screechers, jumping jacks and rockets burst above the town, raining down in showers of red and yellow and white light. I almost laughed out loud. It was a damn clever diversion. The Ross kids obviously thought they were under some sort of paramilitary attack and went into blind panic. While they were screaming and running for cover, diving behind parked cars and into doorways, I could see two, three ... no, five trawlers creeping towards the harbour. By the time everyone realised the explosions were just harmless firecrackers the entire Carrig Cove fishing fleet was only yards from the harbour wall.

Flash, flash, flash. Flash, flash.

Six boats in the water now, lights blazing, like pirate ships about to lay waste to the town.

What are they doing? I thought. *They're never going to attempt to dock? There'll be a right brawl if they do that!*

'Come on,' Conor said to JJ. 'We need to get down there or we'll miss the action.' He tossed his cigarette butt into the ditch and set off at a run, with JJ on his heels.

Conor was right. If Dog and the fishermen were going to rescue Rinn they'd have to come and get him, and if I wanted to see it happen I'd need to be a lot closer than this. I knew the perfect viewing spot, a derelict storehouse in the harbour that I used whenever I felt like skipping school.

I ran down the church steps and grabbed my bicycle from inside the wall. As I lifted it through the gates I saw the heap of abandoned bikes. Most had been dumped on the roadside, but one had been propped carefully against an old tree stump. I'd know it anywhere; a Raleigh Chopper with a lightning flash sticker on the head tube.

Conor McNessa's bike.

There was a rusty nail lying on the road a few inches from the front wheel. I had a sudden urge, which I decided not to bother resisting. I picked up the nail and shoved it into the tyre, dragging a grand gash through the rubber. I'd like to have smashed some spokes while I was at it but I didn't. Let him think the torn tyre was accidental; I'd know different. I tossed the nail into the ditch.

I got on my own bike and headed into town. I went the long way round, avoiding the road Conor and JJ had taken, keeping a sharp lookout for stray Carrig Cove lads as I went.

28
Gus

Getting into the old warehouse was no problem; the lock was still broken from my last visit. I took the light off my bike and went inside.

I climbed the stairs to the third floor and went over to one of the windows. The harbour had been lit up like a stage when I left the church steps. Now, as I stuck my head through the empty window frame, the trawlers cut their lights. The figures around the pier – Maeve and her pals – emerged from their hiding places slowly. I could see them weaving their heads about like a pack of gophers, struggling to adjust their eyes to the dim orange of the halogen lights, trying to figure out what had just happened.

'There's someone out there in the water,' Maeve yelled.

Dog, I thought. *Has to be Dog. Dog, swimming into the harbour to get Rinn.*

'They can't get into the harbour.' Ali's voice. 'The nets will stop them.'

So I was right. They'd attached nets under the pontoons.

'Or this damn thing will kill them.' Another voice, Ratty McRoth's. 'It's going feckin' crazy.'

I strained to make out what was happening inside the enclosed harbour. Someone on the pier wall flicked on a torch and shone it down, and someone in the boat did the same. Rinn was careening in circles, making violent clacking and buzzing sounds. The water was roiling and the skiff with Ali, Ned and Ratty in it was bobbing violently.

Jesus, I thought. *Rinn's going berserk. If Dog gets past the nets he's mince meat.*

I wanted to call out, warn him, but he wouldn't hear anything under water. And he couldn't see. He was basically swimming blind.

Jesus, Jesus. What the hell is he thinking? Where are you, Dog? Come up for air, show yourself.

Then I saw a figure sneaking across the pier. Slight and quick, dripping water.

Dog.

He'd swum from the trawlers to the steps on the

far side of the pier wall and climbed them. While the kids on the pier watched the drama within the harbour, I watched Dog cross the stones a few feet behind them. He stole steadily towards the steps which ran down into the basin. He must have heard what Ali said but he was going in anyway.

'Oi!' Someone spotted Dog on the steps. 'Stop him!'

Too late. Dog slipped into the water, like a seal off a rock.

I held my breath. Suddenly Rinn jerked his tail high out of the water and thrashed it down like a bucking bronco. The watchers on the pier screamed in fright. Rinn's tail shot up, smashed down. Again. Again. Rinn was creating his very own storm in the harbour and the boats in it were bobbing like crazy. The skiff was surely going to tip its crew out any moment. I couldn't see Dog in the churning water.

Someone in the skiff attempted to stand, grabbing for a tyre hanging from the side of one of the moored boats – Ned Cranny, I guessed. Ali tried to pull him back down but he wasn't fast enough. A wave from Rinn's tail struck the boat and over it went. More shouts and screams from the onlookers on the pier.

The skiff flipped upright again, empty. It crashed into the pier, rebounded into the harbour and took a belt of Rinn's tail. Chunks of wood flew into the air. The contact seemed to momentarily stun Rinn. He stopped the violent tail-thrashing, went back to high-speed circling. Torch beams flew across the water, searching for heads.

The three boys surfaced, coughing and spluttering. They struggled to the pier wall as fast as they could, fighting the suck and lash of the waves, one of them barely making it out of Rinn's path in time.

Dog! Jesus, Dog. I hung out that window, frantically trying to spot him.

The three Ross boys had made it to what was left of the skiff and were trying to keep it between them and the crazed animal. And . . . there! I saw Dog, swimming close to the far wall, edging himself along it, moving steadily towards the pontoons.

Rinn seemed to calm slightly, still circling but less wildly. On the pier Maeve straightened up and looked around her. I followed her gaze and saw what she saw – someone in the water beyond the pontoons. Was it a girl? It looked like a girl. Maeve said nothing, didn't point or bring anyone's attention to the swimmer, but by the turn of her head and that of the swimmer, I'd swear their eyes must have locked. After a moment the swimmer looked away. She slapped the surface of the water with her hands.

Rinn's response was immediate. He swam straight over to the barrier. His head broke the surface and he appeared to me to be looking at the swimmer on the other side.

Meanwhile Dog had hauled himself up onto one of the pontoons. As soon as he stood upright the trawlers switched their lights on and the harbour was ablaze again. Dog motioned to Rinn with his arm, drawing an arc in the air, his message clear.

Jump.

I heard Maeve's mocking laugh.

Rinn disappeared below the surface.

Everyone, everything, went still. I held my breath.

Come on Rinn, I thought. *Do it. Do it for Dog, do it for Carrig Cove.*

There was an explosion of sound and water.

The dolphin was in the air, flying over the pontoons, over Dog, escaping into the bay.

'Yes!' I yelled. 'Yes, yes, yes!'

Dog dived after Rinn. The trawlers sounded their horns and rang their bells to signal the victory of Carrig Cove. The noise was deafening. Up in the cheap seats I gave them a standing ovation. I hollered and clapped and yelled. What a grand finale.

Down on the pier the rest of the audience was stunned. The Ross kids watched, hands hanging, as the dolphin and its rescuers got away. Maeve was the only one to react. She took her hands from her hips and clapped slowly, shaking her head in disbelief as Dog and the girl were hauled on board the *Ella Louise*.

The Carrig Cove trawlers backed and turned in formation, some manoeuvres performed in unison, others done in almost perfect sequence. One of the skippers must have been roaring instructions over the radio and the rest scrambling to follow them, but, my god, did it look impressive from on shore. The boats left, still honking their derision. Rinn rippled alongside them into the bay.

Show's over folks. You can all go home.

29
Emer

I kept my gaze fixed on Rinn as we pulled away from Ross. He settled into the wake of the *Ella Lou* and followed like a lamb, even though we hadn't as much as a sprat to offer him. The moonlight caught his eye each time he surfaced. It glittered at me before he went under again, down into the inky wash. I longed to look at Dog, to ask if he was all right, but his eyes were black and distant and his body was clenched like a fist. I focused on Rinn.

'Come on, Rinn, come on. Stay with us,' I whispered. 'They will only trap you again if you go back.'

I was shivering from the dowsing in Ross harbour. I'd dragged my clothes on as soon as Dan and Jim hauled us back on board and now my jeans and

T-shirt were stuck to me like a clammy sealskin. Goosebumps spread across my arms, and my teeth began to chatter uncontrollably. It wasn't just the cold. I was buzzing with adrenaline. I was breathing too quickly, my heart was hammering. I couldn't get my head around what we'd done. Had we really sailed out like a band of warriors and tracked our summer visitor through the night to Ross? Had we really taken him back, right there, right in front of our rival town, and left his kidnappers gawping as we sailed away?

So this is why people climb high mountains. This is why people jump out of planes, I thought. *For this. For this.*

I'd played my part. Rinn had gone crazy when he realised he was trapped. I'd had to fight for his attention. Of the Ross crowd I was pretty sure only Maeve Grogan spotted me in the water. She looked straight at me. I'd swear I saw her smile.

'Dog,' Dan said behind me. 'Would you put this jumper on Emer? She's shaking to bits.'

I kept my watch on Rinn. I didn't turn my head till Dog sat down beside me. He was himself again, his eyes back to their normal colours. He had Dan's jumper in his arms.

'We did it,' he said. 'We damn well did it.'

I nodded and laughed, Dog's dimples flashing at

me as he laughed back. He dumped Dan's enormous Aran over my head and I was swallowed up. The wool smelled of fish and diesel.

'Are you in there somewhere?' he said, tugging at the tail of the jumper till my head came through the top.

I giggled and he grabbed me around the waist, armfuls of Aran and all. 'Woohoo!' he yelled. 'Carrig Cove, *abú*!'

'Carrig Cove, *abú*!' yelled Dan and Jim.

Our whoops echoed out across the bay and answering calls came back to us from the other trawlers. Rinn caught our excitement and breached, jumping straight up like an arrow, as if he was reaching for the big yellow moon above our heads. For a few moments the bay was filled with yells and horns blaring. The celebrations echoed around the cliffs and bounced back to us as Rinn disappeared beneath the waves.

Dog climbed onto the bench behind me, straddling it so his legs surrounded me. I leaned back into him and he pressed his head against mine, and we watched our dolphin follow us back to Carrig Cove as if he was tethered to the *Ella Lou* with an invisible rope. It was nearly two in the morning. It was dark. We were returning home, conquering heroes in a flotilla of war boats.

'The village is asleep,' I said to Dog as we got close to shore. 'It doesn't know it should be out on the pier, cheering. There should be a brass band and flags.'

He grinned. 'They'll know soon enough,' he said. 'It'll be all over the place first thing tomorrow morning.'

I froze. 'Da,' I said. 'My da can't know I was involved. He'd kill me.'

'But you helped get his moneymaker back,' Dog said. 'He should be thrilled.'

'And how did I end up out in the middle of the night? And with you?'

'Right.' Dog bit his lip.

'I can't be part of the story, Dog,' I said. 'I wasn't here.'

He nodded.

'Will you tell Dan and Jim, make them understand?'

He nodded again. 'If you're sure. You could brazen it out with your da. What's the worst that could happen?'

'He grounds me for the rest of the summer,' I said. 'He decides he won't let me go to college next year. He locks me in my room and throws away the key.'

'And you'd climb out the window, like you do now,' Dog said.

I laughed but the thought of Da knowing made me queasy. Oh, he'd put on a bright smile for the village but I knew just how horrible he'd be to me once the shop door was closed.

Rinn peeled off as we entered the harbour. I lifted a hand in salute. Dog kissed my cheek. The *Ella Lou* was the first to dock. Jim was about to jump off with a rope when we saw women emerging from the shadows, the fishermen's women: Dan's wife Stella, Jim's sister Delia, Mrs Cox, Mrs Roche, Mary's granny, old Mrs Ryan. We had a welcoming committee after all.

'You did it?' Stella said, as she caught the rope Jim tossed. 'You brought Rinn home?'

'Aye,' Dan said. 'The youngsters here got him back for us.'

I saw Stella and Delia peering into the boat to see who he meant. I ducked behind Dog. 'I'm not here, Dan,' I hissed. 'I can't be here. Da can't know I was part of this.'

Dan pulled a face and Dog shielded me from sight. 'Dog, it was,' he said. 'Dog did it, and Kit and the other lads created a fine diversion with their firecrackers. They'll be back across the causeway soon, I'm sure.'

I crept into the wheelhouse while the boat was tied

up and the women dispersed to help secure the other trawlers as they came in.

'Paudy has the bar open,' I heard Stella say to Dan. 'He has pints pulled and the kettle boiled for hot whiskeys.'

'Dog, too?' Jim asked. 'There'll be no celebrating without him.'

'You can work that out with Paudy,' Stella said. 'I don't see him objecting. You know Paudy. This will be the story to end all stories and he'll be wanting to hear every last detail of it ten times before sunup.'

Dog hung back as the fishermen stepped off the boat.

'You'll follow us over once you've seen Emer home?' Dan said to him in a low voice.

Dog nodded. He slipped inside the wheelhouse and we stood together in the shadows. We watched as Stella kissed her man. She gave Jim a kiss on the cheek for good measure. We hid our giggles in Dan's enormous jumper. Dog's hands stole beneath it and he stroked my still damp skin. I turned my face to him and our lips met. We kissed and touched with half the village only yards away from us, all kissing and touching. Dog's lips on my lips, my face, my neck, his hands in my hair, on my stomach, my back, my breasts, as the voices of the men and women drifted away.

‘The other night.’ he asked. ‘Were you OK? After what . . . happened between us?’

I nodded. ‘I was, I am,’ I whispered.

‘I’d rather stay here with you than go drinking in Paudy’s,’ he said.

‘Fibber,’ I said, and he laughed.

‘All right,’ he said. ‘I want to be here with you as much as I want to go and have my first official pint in Paudy’s.’

I knew at that moment I had the power to make him stay. I only had to say the words.

‘See me home and then go have your pint,’ I said. ‘They’ll start the story without you if we don’t get a move on.’

We stepped out of the cabin and onto the pier. As we got to the street we heard the rattle of a bicycle and Kit came up behind us.

‘Did Rinn follow you back?’ he said, struggling to catch his breath.

‘He did. He’s home,’ Dog said. ‘Where’s Conor and the rest of them?’

Kit scowled. ‘It wasn’t enough for Conor that you got Rinn out of the trap,’ he said. ‘He decided Ross needed to be taught a lesson. The hullabaloo brought half the town rushing down to the harbour to see what was going on so there was a big crowd there by the time the trawlers were pulling away. We snuck up the hill to get back to our bikes and get the hell out of Dodge before anyone spotted us. That's when Conor and the others decided there was more to be done. They went on a rampage, smashing windows, slashing car tyres, pushing over anything that'd break. I told them to quit it but they wouldn't, so I left them to it and came home.'

'Conor McNessa is an arsehole,' a voice said.

We turned to see Fee standing there, rumpled and wiping sleep from her eyes. 'Stella wouldn't let me wait with her and the women. She told me to go home but I wasn't missing ye coming back. I sat on the bench beside the phone box. I must have dozed off. What did I miss?'

'I wish you'd seen it, Fee,' Kit said. 'It was fabulous. The diversion worked like a charm. Frightened the shite out of the Rossers. Ali Matthews and his pals fell out of their boat and Dog swam into the harbour when they weren't looking and next thing he's standing on their poxy barricades and Rinn is soaring out of the trap they'd made. He jumped right over Dog's head. It was magic.'

Fee pulled a face. 'I'd like to have seen that,' she said.

'You helped make it happen,' Dog said. 'We

wouldn't have made it with just the *Ella Lou*. The other trawlers tipped the balance. The Rossers knew they were out-gunned.'

'Where are all the men?' Kit asked. 'Where are Dan and Jim?'

'Paudy is having a lock-in in our honour,' Dog said. 'Free pints and hot whiskey for the conquering heroes.'

'Are we invited?'

'We are,' Dog said.

'Let's go then,' Kit said. 'Jesus, what a night. We stick it to Ross in high style and you and me finally get to put our feet under the bar at Paudy's. I've been dreaming about doing that since I was ten.' He kissed Fee and began to wheel his bike over to the pub. 'Come on,' he said. 'Conor and his gang will miss it and it serves them right.'

Dog looked at me.

'Go on,' I said. 'Fee and me can walk ourselves home.' I gave him a push. He grinned and kissed me and ran after Kit. I fought the urge to call him back.

He'll never be all mine, I thought. *He'll always belong in the world of men more than he'll ever belong to me.*

'Pints and whiskeys for the conquering heroes,' Fee said, rolling her eyes. 'And we don't even get a mangy packet of crisps, because we're girls.'

'You know Paudy Bán's is a men-only zone,' I said.

'Yeah, right, but Paudy sends his wife in to clean up first thing every morning,' Fee said. 'OK. I need the gory details now.'

'Tomorrow,' I said. 'I need to get into bed before my folks notice I'm gone, and so do you.'

'You're joking?'

'I'm not,' I said. 'I'll have to be up first thing tomorrow – today – to do a day's work. This is the only thing anyone will be talking about. I can't have Da guessing I was part of it.'

She nodded. 'OK. But I'll want to hear everything.'

We stopped at the side gate. She hugged me.

'Are you all right?' she whispered, scanning my face, suddenly alert to my mood.

'I'm grand,' I said. 'I just need to come down. It was insane.'

And I needed to swallow my ridiculous disappointment at how easily Dog walked away from me to be with Kit and the men, to soak up the acclaim of being the hero. Sure, hadn't I told him to go? This was who Dog was – did I really want him to be someone else for me?

III

30
Gus

'It was you, right?' The husky voice in the shadows of the hotel yard could only belong to one girl.

I lit my cigarette. 'What was?' I said.

'The other night,' she said. 'You went over to Carrig Cove and told Dog Cullen what I was up to.' She stepped out into the light and regarded me with one eyebrow raised. 'I won't tell on you. I'd just like you to admit it. I'd prefer to keep things straight between us.'

'Us?' I snorted. 'There is no us. You got what you wanted, now leave me alone.'

She laughed. 'You think I slept with you so you'd take Ned and Ratty over to that kip you love so much? Honey lamb, you'd have done that for a smile and the hint of a kiss. I slept with you because I wanted to. And I want to again.'

I blushed in the dark. Jesus, but she had balls. What was a guy to do?

'It was you?' she said again.

'It was me.'

She reached up and took the cigarette from my mouth.

'It was something else, wasn't it? Something to remember when all of us have mortgages and kids. One summer we stole a dolphin and nearly got away with it.'

She put my cigarette between her lips, took a long drag, then placed it back between mine.

'And that rescue. That was something too. Didn't know the wee folk of Carrig had it in them. The trawlers, the fireworks, dolphin leaping over boy to freedom – I was impressed. It was almost worth watching all my plans unravel.'

My turn to laugh, in surprise.

She shrugged. 'I got what I wanted,' she said. 'Publicity.' She jerked her head towards the hotel behind us where the dining room was buzzing. 'It's wall-to-wall journalists in there tonight,' she said. 'Some of them are from the nationals. The telly people are coming tomorrow to do a piece for the evening news. A dolphin in the bay is a good story. Two towns going to war over it, now that's a great story.

Ross is back on the map, Carrig has its precious fish, everyone's happy.'

'What were you going to do with him?' I said. 'If you'd managed to hold onto him?'

'This, pretty much,' she said. 'Photocalls and interviews for a few days, then let him go. If he switched allegiance to Ross it would've been a bonus. I knew we couldn't keep him in the harbour forever.'

I shook my head. 'You're quite something yourself, Maeve Grogan,' I said.

'Gus, where in hell are you?' The roar came from the kitchen. 'These dishes won't wash themselves.'

'Gotta go,' I said, offering her the last of my ciggy. 'Can't keep Hannibal waiting.'

'I'm not much for waiting myself,' she said. 'So don't be late tonight.'

I stared at her.

'All the rooms are full,' she said, taking a long drag. 'It'll have to be the beach. I'll meet you there after your shift ends. Bring a blanket.'

'A blanket? How am I—'

'You'll think of something,' she said and walked away, crushing the end of my cigarette against the walls as she went.

31
Gus

The night was stiflingly close and still, even on the beach. We made love on a blanket I nicked from the hotel store cupboard. Afterwards we raced each other into the sea to wash off the sweat and sand. I watched the water stream down Maeve's naked body, watched her shake her hair about her shoulders with all the unconscious grace of a cat. We dried ourselves with hotel towels I'd had the foresight to pinch along with the blanket. I walked Maeve back to Main Street and left her with one last lingering kiss.

It was three in the morning – I had to remind myself not to whistle my way up Tavern Street. I stopped wanting to when I rounded the corner and saw what was scrawled across my front door.

GUS MCROY
TRAITOR
AND
THIEF

The words were slathered on in gloss paint, that sickly shade of green that's almost brown. It was still sticky and dripping. Mam had only painted the door bright red that spring. I walked around the side of the house into the yard to fetch some turps and a rag. I stopped in my tracks again.

Even in the half-light I could see my car was too low. I leaned down and sure enough, the wheels, all four, had been slashed.

Conor McNessa, I thought. *You bollocks. You piece of shite.*

I knew it was him, I just knew. He and his crew of baboons had done a rake of damage before they left Ross the night of the rescue, including a heap of slashed car tyres. Tonight Conor had come back especially to add me to his hit list.

Replacing four tyres would cost me a bloody fortune. Goldie would be on blocks for weeks and I'd be back on my bike. I felt rage course through me. It wasn't fair. It wasn't fucking fair. Without me Carrig Cove wouldn't have known their dolphin was gone till it was too late, and here I was being branded a traitor. And a thief too, as if I'd taken part in Maeve's crazy raid.

I set to cleaning the door, taking out my frustration on the task. Fuck Carrig Cove, fuck Ross. I didn't belong to either. I couldn't wait till next year. They wouldn't see my heels for dust. As for Conor McNessa, I'd get even with him. I'd get even or die trying.

32
Emer

For days it was all anyone talked about. Carrig basked in the glory of the Great Dolphin Rescue. Everyone walked around smiling. Rinn was 'our' dolphin, 'our' Rinn. Dog was the hero, Dan and the other men had a skip in their step. Dan was good as his word. He made sure Stella and the fishermen knew not to mention my name when they were telling and retelling the story. Da never suspected a thing and if Mam did, she never said.

But three days in, the gloss began to come off our victory. Maeve Grogan's father went on TV, laughed the whole think off as a prank and said people should come and see the 'Ross Bay' dolphin for themselves. The TV people crossed the causeway to Carrig but they only shot fifteen minutes of film and left without talking to anyone, as if they'd already heard everything they needed to know over in Ross. Carrig was presented on telly as a backwater full of country yokels who'd be as likely to shake a pitchfork at you as tip their caps.

And the reprisals began, reprisals for the damage Conor and the other lads had done that night after the rescue. We woke up one morning to find every window box in the village stinking of vinegar and the flowers throwing themselves over the sides. That might have been the end of it but Conor wouldn't call it quits. He led a gang across to Ross the next night and they destroyed the flowerbeds on the green. Every few days since then some sort of damage was done.

At first all the tit-for-tat happened at night but then the lads in Carrig set up night patrols to catch the pranksters and Ross did the same. The Ross kids got clever and began doing their dirty work in broad daylight, sending in lone operators disguised as dolphin visitors. Conor and the lads couldn't do the same in Ross so tempers were running high as they tried to stay ahead in the revenge game.

Dog and Kit had nothing to do with the messing. Their spare time was spent with Fee and me, and Rinn. We had settled back into the rhythm of our night swims; all was good with the world. A few weeks after the rescue there was this one night when Rinn was acting a bit frisky. Fee and me got out after a few minutes and left the boys to it. We flopped down on the sand and I raised an arm over my head and traced the Milky Way with my finger.

Fee rolled over onto her stomach. 'How are things with you and Dog?' she asked.

'Grand,' I said. I smiled. 'Lovely, actually.'

'Lovely? What does that mean? You haven't—? No, of course you haven't. But I have. Me and Kit. We've done it. We're being careful, of course. I wouldn't let him go all the way till he did a trip across the border to buy some johnnies.' She laughed but she sounded nervous. 'Do you think I'm a slut?'

'Do you seriously think I'd think that? Jesus, Fee.' I reached across and hugged her. 'You'll always be my Fee, my best friend.' She held me close for a moment and we rocked each other.

'All right,' she said. 'Enough of that,' and she pulled away and swiped her nose with her wrist. 'What's the latest news on the street? Who did what this week?'

'The latest?' I said. 'The latest is that someone slipped rat poison in our gobstopper dispenser.'

'You're joking?' Fee said. 'The one outside the door?'

'Yep. A woman came in yelling about it this evening – she'd spotted the bits of poison on a gobstopper as her kid was about to shove it in his mouth.'

'Jesus! Did your da go mad?'

'You can imagine. He was so furious he kicked the dispenser. It toppled over and the glass smashed. The gobstoppers went everywhere. There was a bunch of little kids hanging around and they were on them like lightning, stuffing their pockets full. I had to chase after them to warn them to not to eat them.'

'I'm surprised your da didn't want them back.' She snorted. 'Molly's Tearooms has had to close. Someone reported Molly to the food and health. Apparently you need a licence to serve tea and cakes in your front garden. I suspect the someone who reported her came from over yonder and their da drives a silver Merc.' She nodded in the general direction of Ross. 'Mrs Ryan got cautioned for running an unregistered B&B. It's all revenge for us getting Rinn back.'

'Ross are definitely getting one over on Conor and the lads,' I said. 'Conor likes to smash and destroy. The Ross lot have pushed it to a whole other level.'

'I heard Conor's gang are planning something big tonight. They're probably over there sneaking around as we speak. You know what I think?' She sat up. 'I think he wants some of the glory. He thinks the world of Dog, I'll give him that, but he can't stand playing second fiddle to anyone. You'd think the firework diversion was all his doing, his idea. It was Kit suggested it and Kit who had the fireworks and Kit who handed them out and suggested where they let them off, but you'd never know that from the way Conor tells the story.' She leaned forward and peered at the waves in the dark. 'What was that? Did one of them shout?'

'I don't think so,' I said, sitting up and narrowing my eyes to try and locate Kit and Dog in the water.

Then there was an unmistakable yell, a roar of pain.

'That's Kit,' Fee said, and we both leapt to our feet.

'My leg, my leg,' Kit shouted. 'He belted my leg. I can't . . .'

We spotted him as he went under. I could see Dog already swimming over as I waded in.

'There!' I shouted, pointing to where I'd seen Kit go down.

Dog dived and came back up almost immediately with Kit spluttering in his arms. As he swam towards us, one arm crooked around Kit's neck I saw a fin bearing down on the two boys.

'No, Rinn,' I yelled. I slapped the surface of the water.

The fin slowed down. I swam forward quickly, got myself almost level with Dog and Kit and slapped the water again.

'Go away, Rinn,' I shouted. 'Leave.'

Rinn clacked his beak at me but he turned and moved away, out into the bay. I swam to Dog and together we pulled Kit into shallow water, found our feet and got him to his. The three of us watched the disappearing fin.

When we reached the beach Kit collapsed onto the stones, groaning. 'Jesus, my leg,' he said. 'Christ, it hurts, it hurts like hell.'

Fee peeled his fingers back from his thigh and even in the darkness we could see a huge bruise blooming.

'Do you think it's broken?' she asked.

Kit shook his head. 'If he'd hit me below the knee, it'd be a different story,' he said through gritted teeth.

Fee nodded but we could all see how much pain Kit was in. He rocked back and forth and screwed up his eyes to stop tears leaking down his cheeks.

'Give me a few minutes,' he said. 'Let me catch my breath.'

Fee sat down beside him and he leaned over, so

he was half lying in her lap. 'Was that an accident out there?' she said. 'Or did Rinn attack you?'

Kit frowned. 'It seemed . . . it seemed like he came at me. Like he meant it. But it happened so quickly.'

'What do we do?' Fee said. 'Do we tell someone? Because if Rinn's becoming unfriendly someone could get hurt.'

'Hey,' Kit said, throwing a hand in the air. 'Someone is hurt.'

'You know what I mean,' Fee said. 'What if he went for a kid, or attacked one of the boats and knocked people overboard?'

They all looked at me, like I should have the answer.

'We talk to Dan,' I said. 'Dan'll know what to do. Right now, we need to get Kit home.'

The three of us half-carried Kit up the beach, then Fee and me helped Dog get Kit to the Cullens' house. It was further away than Kit's, but Dog said his mother would have something to sort the pain and she wouldn't ask too many questions. Lights were already snapping on inside as Fee and me left them at the door. I heard Dee Cullen's voice saying, 'Goodness me, what have you lads been up to this time?'

33

Emer

Next morning the shop was barely open when I saw Fee beckon me through the window.

'Just going outside for a breath of air, Da,' I said. 'Won't be long.' I walked out before he could answer.

Fee and Dog were waiting a few doors up the street. Rory was there too, hanging back a couple of feet behind Dog.

'Hey Ror,' I said. 'Haven't seen you in ages.' I turned to the other two. 'Let's do this,' I said.

We'd agreed last night that we'd tell Dan what had happened with Rinn as soon as we could. Dan and Jim were over on the pier getting the *Ella Lou* ready for the day's outings. The first punters were already climbing onto the *Dulcie*, tickets in hand.

As we got closer we could see there was

something wrong. Patsy Roche and Martin Cox were staring at the lobster pots stacked against the pier wall. The men looked up as we reached them, their faces angry.

'What's happened?' Dog said.

'Those hooligans from Ross were here last night,' Dan said, keeping his voice low so the day trippers wouldn't hear. 'Serious damage this time.' He pointed to the wall where the words 'Go Fish' had been painted in crude lettering. Patsy pulled a lobster pot from the stack and held it up so we could see where it had been snipped with cutters in several places.

'They're all damaged,' Martin said. 'Some worse than others but they got every last one of them, and they've had a go at the nets and all.'

Dan lifted the edge of a net, hauled it across the pier and he and Jim began examining it, stretching lengths of it out between them. Patsy sucked in his teeth when he saw the holes that'd been made.

'That'll take some mending,' he said. 'You youngsters think it's just a bit of monkey business but it's not you has to do the fixing.' His voice got sharper as he spoke.

'Hey, hey,' Jim said. 'It's not their fault, Patsy. They haven't been up to anything, have ye?'

Dog shook his head. 'Neither me nor Kit,' he said,

'but I can't answer for everyone. There has been stuff done, over in Ross.'

'So I heard,' Dan said. 'It needs to stop. It's getting out of hand. This is serious damage. Put the word out. This nonsense ends. Now.'

Dog nodded. He turned and walked up the pier.

Fee looked at me. 'What about—'

I shook my head. It didn't seem like a good time to mention that Rinn, the golden alternative to fishing, was showing signs of going rogue. We followed Dog back to the street. When we caught up with him I could see he was furious.

'Dan's right,' he said. 'This stuff Conor and the lads have been doing, this messing, it's got to stop. It's a coward's game. We should sort it out properly, face to face, like men. Today.'

Fee and myself looked at each other. I opened my mouth to say something but Dog's face was closed tight, his eyes were looking inwards. He walked away from Fee and me as if we weren't there. I said nothing. There was no point, no point arguing with Dog, no point in saying 'Don't fight. It's not the answer'. Whatever he was going to do, he'd do it, and nothing I said would stop him.

34
Gus

'It's make your mind up time, Gus. Chose a side: Carrig Cove or Ross. You can't be on both.' Maeve had a piece of paper in her hand. She held it up in front of my face.

'This ends today,' it read. 'Your lot against ours. Ladies' Nook, four o'clock. Dog Cullen.'

'D'you know what they did last night?' Maeve said. 'They came over here and broke into the hotel yard. Syphoned off half a keg of beer and pissed in at least one of the barrels. My father had to ditch the lot. A fortune's worth of booze, down the drain.'

'I heard there was some pretty bad damage done over there too,' I said, looking at Ali.

He shrugged. 'So we rowed over and cut up a few nets. They're hardly using them these days anyway – too busy with their dolphin trips.'

'They're still fishing. Nets and pots take serious man-hours and money to repair,' I said. 'I'd say the damage is pretty even.'

'And I say your friend Dog is right,' Maeve said. 'It's time to finish this, face to face. Are you with us or not?' She and Ali stared at me, waiting.

'I won't fight Dog,' I said. 'But promise me Conor McNessa and I'll show you whose side I'm on.'

'Good man,' Ali said, slapping me on the shoulder. 'I told you he'd come around,' he said to Maeve.

I frowned but didn't comment on his choice of words.

'How many?' Maeve said. 'How many Carrig Cove boys will there be?'

I did a quick tot in my head. 'I'd say ten, possibly eleven.'

She nodded. 'That's what we figured. We've got ten, once we have you.'

'Don't suppose that brother of yours is back from Dublin yet?' Ali said. 'No? Damn. He'd have been the ace in the pack. Who from their side's going to be most dangerous? The Cullen guy, I presume.'

I nodded. 'Easily. There are a couple of lefties – Kit Crosby and Phelim Roche. JJ O'Toole will be their weakest fighter, so I'd pit Peter or Tony against him.'

Ali smiled at me. 'That's really useful to know,

Gus,' he said. He slapped my shoulder again and I forced a smile. Behind his back Maeve winked at me.

'Ladies' Nook,' she said, 'is that the tiny beach halfway along the cliff road?'

'It is,' I said. 'Women swam there in the old days because it's hidden from the road and has a cave they could change in. No one goes there now. I suppose that's why Dog chose it.'

'How long will it take us to cycle there? Twenty minutes?'

'About.'

'Right,' she said. 'We'll assemble at the post office at three-thirty, leave at three-forty exactly.' She smiled. 'We'll let them get there first. That way we'll make an entrance and have the battle half won before it even begins.'

35
Gus

As we began the descent to the beach I understood why Maeve had been so intent on arriving second. She organised us in the lay-by, made us get into twos: the girls first, then the lads. Every girl was wearing a long dress, presumably on Maeve's instructions. Maeve herself had on a flowing thing, deep aqua green at the hem fading to pale sky blue as it rose up to her neck. It clung to her body and swished around her ankles. She wore bird earrings, delicate and golden, which dangled just above her shoulders.

To the watchers on the beach below we must have looked like a column of soldiers marching to victory. We developed a rhythm as we walked down the narrow winding stairs, our feet tramping: step, down, step, down, step, down. None of us turned our heads to peek at the beach through the marram grass. We were on show and we maintained the theatre of it all the way down.

When Maeve raised her hand to call us to a halt it was a shock to see only five people waiting – Dog, Kit Crosby, Emer Monaghan, Fee Hennessy and a red-headed kid I presumed was Fee's brother. There were twenty-one of us, five of them.

Where are the rest of the Carrig Cove boys? I thought. *Where the hell is Conor Mc-fecking-Nessa?*

Kit came forward and I saw he was limping. He hobbled halfway across the beach and waited. Maeve turned her head slightly.

'Ratty,' she said, and Ratty McRoth who was directly behind me in the conga line, stepped out and edged his way down the steps past the rest of us. He adopted a sloping walk as he crossed the sand, trying to act cool with everyone's eyes on him.

Kit began to speak, his voice too low for us to hear him. Ratty answered him, then Kit limped back to Dog. A few minutes later he came over to Ratty again, said something into his ear and Ratty returned to Maeve.

'They won't talk to me,' he said. 'It has to be him.' He jerked his head towards me. Maeve nodded. I walked down the steps and crossed the sand. My turn to act nonchalant.

'What the fuck?' I whispered to Kit. 'Where's Conor? Where's Phelim and JJ? Where is everyone?'

'You heard what they did last night?' Kit said. 'About the kegs of beer at the Bay View?'

I nodded.

'Well, they could only carry so much, so they drank a load while they were there and guzzled what they took on the way back. They were paralytic. I'm surprised they even made it home. Right now, they're all laid up with hangovers the size of Tyrone, trying to convince their mammies it's a mass outbreak of food poisoning. Dog didn't know about it when he issued the challenge or we'd have set it for tomorrow.'

'Is that what you're suggesting?' I asked. 'That we do this tomorrow? Because I can't see it flying with this lot.' I rolled my eyes back towards the steps.

Kit shook his head. 'I tried to convince Dog to do that but it's just too much face to lose.'

'You two can't take us all on,' I said. 'You don't look up to much, if you don't mind me saying, and that kid with the girls must be about ten.' I glanced over at the small group standing in front of the cliff. 'What'd you do to yourself, anyway?'

'I came off my bike,' Kit said. 'Here's what Dog proposes. He takes on three of you, one by one, and the best of three wins.'

'Wins what?'

'Custody of Rinn. And this tit-for-tat stuff stops. Will you put it to them?' Kit looked over my shoulder at the Ross kids, massed on the cliff steps, silently watching and waiting.

'I will,' I said. 'Jaysus, Kit, he's some fella, is Dog. I came here today to beat the shite out of Conor, but I'll be rooting for Dog, you know that?'

'We were surprised to see you coming down the steps,' Kit said. 'D'you not think it's time to let it go, this thing between yourself and Conor? Ye were kids, for feck's sake.'

'Tell that to Conor,' I said. 'He came over to Ross last week and painted a load of bull across my ma's front door and slashed my car tyres into the bargain.'

'Seriously?' Kit frowned. 'I get where you're coming from, so. But you'll make the case for hand to hand, one at a time with Dog?'

'I will,' I said. We shook on it and I walked back across the sand to Maeve. Ali had made his way down to stand beside her.

'The rest of the Carrig lads are laid up,' I said. 'They drank too much of your father's beer last night, and Kit there has banjaxed his leg, so Dog proposes to do all the fighting himself, one at a time, best of three.'

Ali was about to protest but Maeve cut him with a look. 'Best of five,' she said, her voice ringing out across the sand, loud enough for everyone to hear, including Dog and the others on the beach. 'Agreed?'

I saw Emer's eyes widen in alarm. She made to reach for Dog's arm but Fee pulled her away, back to the shadows, towards the cave.

Dog nodded to Kit. 'Agreed,' Kit shouted.

'Good,' Maeve said. 'And the fighters from Ross will be . . . Ned, Ratty, Gus, Dave and Ali. In that order.'

I opened my mouth to protest and she arched an eyebrow. I glared at her but I knew as well as she did that I couldn't refuse to fight, not in front of every single kid I knew, not if I ever wanted to hold my head up again in either of the places I called home.

36
Gus

We agreed rules – bare feet, fists only, above the belt only. No biting, no spitting, no tripping, no kicking, no headbutting. A knockout or three knock-downs for one fighter finished the fight. After five minutes the fight would be halted and whoever had gone down the most times or taken the most hits was the loser. Kit and Maeve would keep the score. There'd be three minutes' rest between fights.

Kit and I marked out a rough square in the sand and placed rolled up sweatshirts at its corners. The Ross kids came down onto the beach and formed a semi-circle to watch. Emer and Fee and the red-haired kid stayed where they were, at the mouth of the cave. Kit stood beside Dog, ready to send him in. I went and stood with Ali and the other chosen few. We made a show of warming up, stretching our legs, punching the air and assembling our fighting faces.

'Time,' Maeve said.

Ned and Dog stripped off their T-shirts to whistles from the watching girls. Ned walked forward and they shook hands. I knew Ned for a slugger. He crouched dead centre of the ring with his fists raised in front of his chin. Dog danced around him, diving in and delivering jabs to Ned's belly and face. Ned took the hits, turning with Dog.

I knew what Ned was doing. He was much bigger than Dog and he could do a lot of damage if he once landed a punch. He had this one move he liked to make and he was waiting for Dog to provide him with the opportunity to make it. But Ned was too slow; he never got his chance. Dog had him on his back within three minutes. Ned got himself a bloody nose and a black eye; he never did land a finger on Dog.

'Time,' Maeve said.

Ratty fared better. He'd done a little boxing in the youth club and he wasn't called Ratty for nothing. He crowded Dog, landed a sharp one in his ribs and another close to his ear before Dog got the measure of him. I saw Dog figuring out Ratty's pattern, his little bob and weave technique. The next time Ratty moved in, Dog faked a left hook. Ratty leaned away to avoid it but Dog had anticipated. He moved with him and delivered a swift uppercut to Ratty's jaw. The watchers groaned as a tooth flew and Ratty hit the sand.

'Your turn next, Gus,' Ali said to me, dancing a little side-to-side and pocketa-pocketa-ing an imaginary punch bag. 'No one will think the worse of you if you throw it. At least, I won't.' He smiled a bland smile. 'I mean, he's your best buddy, right?'

I might have bought his act if he hadn't let his eyes momentarily slide sideways to Maeve. It was the merest flicker, but in that moment I understood. He knew. He knew about Maeve and me.

'Time,' Maeve called.

I stripped off my shirt and walked into the square to face Dog. We shook hands.

'I didn't want this, Dog,' I said, keeping my voice low so only he could hear. 'She called my name before I could stop her.'

Dog nodded. His eyes were focused. I wasn't sure he'd heard what I said.

'If she'd called me first or second I'd have thrown it,' I said, keeping my head down so my fringe masked my mouth. 'But I can't be the one who gives you the win, understand? It can't be me.'

His grin was grim. 'You'd better do your worst

then, Gus,' he said, 'because I've no intention of taking it easy on you.'

And he didn't. Despite the difference in our heights and weights we were well matched. Even with the advantage of being fresh I found it hard going. Sure, I could have gone to work on his left ribs, where Ratty had got him, but I wouldn't stoop that low. I landed a few good ones: his right eye, his jaw, his stomach, and he caught me a jab in mine and bloodied my nose with that left hook of his. After a few minutes we were already fairly sore and tired. I grabbed Dog around the waist and pulled him down, both of us rolling on the sand.

'This is all Conor's fault,' I hissed. 'And the fecker isn't here to take his share.'

'All Conor's fault?' Dog said. 'Not hers?' He jerked his chin towards Maeve. 'Stealing Rinn was her idea.'

I didn't answer, just clenched my lips shut.

'Ah,' Dog said. 'Shagging her, are you?'

We rolled across the sand again, both of us happy to stay down for a few seconds, panting and catching our breaths. The kids were roaring at us and we made a brief show of wrestling each other, rolling ourselves out of the ring.

'Do you do whatever she tells you?' Dog said, his

mouth at my ear. 'Were you with them when they came over and wrecked the nets last night?'

I grabbed a fistful of his hair and pulled his head back so I could look him in the face. 'What do you think?' I growled. 'I don't go in for that sneaking around, smashing things in the dark and running away. Not like that weasel, Conor. Did Kit tell you what he did? To my car, to the house?'

He went to punch me half-heartedly and I pinned his arm. The Ross kids were shouting, 'Gus, Gus, come on Gus.'

'What colour paint was the message on your ma's door?' Dog said. 'Wasn't shite green, was it?'

I stopped struggling. 'How did you know?'

'There was stuff scrawled on the pier wall this morning. Shite green paint,' he said. 'Who led the raid on the nets?'

'Ali,' I said. 'It was Ali.'

TRAITOR AND THIEF. If Ali knew it was me that went over to Carrig to tell Dog they'd kidnapped Rinn, if he knew about Maeve and me, then those words made sense, as much sense as if it was Conor that wrote them. I was so gobsmacked Dog could have sorted me with one good swing but he let me be. He pulled out of my grasp and sprang to his feet. Kit began to count but I was up in three. We walked back into the square and began circling each other. Dog came in quick and I blocked. He came at me again, this time he locked his arms around me as if he was weary. The Ross kids booed.

'I'll let you win,' he whispered, 'but you'll owe me.'

'OK,' I said. And I jabbed him in his stomach.

It wouldn't have hurt much but we were so close together no one would have guessed. Dog doubled up and toppled to the ground. I jumped back and waited.

There was a roar from the Ross kids and Maeve began counting. Dog stayed down. Other than Kit I was the only one who could see his face. It was costing him dear, but he stayed down.

'Nine, ten. Gus wins,' Maeve yelled.

The Ross kids went wild. Kit ran to Dog to help him up. Dog shook him off, got to his feet and walked straight into the sea. I took the hanky Maeve handed me for my nose and she held another up to the cut on my chin.

Watching Dog in the water, clearing his head, I saw the dolphin, out beyond in the bay. Had it been there all along?

Do you know what you've started, Rinn? I thought. *How in hell did I wind up here on this beach, fighting Dog Cullen for the honour of Ross?*

'Time,' Maeve said.

Dave Hannigan walked into the ring, tugging his T-shirt off as he went. Dog came back out of the water. I heard the gasp around me as everyone took in the expression on his face. It was familiar to me. I'd seen it a few times before – in the schoolyard, in the boxing ring, on the GAA field. When Dog got really angry that handsome face of his turned hideous, all popping veins and purple fury. I pitied Dave. I saw the lad blanch. He put his fists up in front of his face.

Dog had to be tired. His knuckles had to be screaming in pain. He was covered in cuts and bruises, there was blood on his skin, on his jeans, in his hair, but he flew at Dave like a madman, dealing out punches at a ferocious pace. I glanced over at Emer and Fee and the young lad standing with them. Emer's face was snow white and she was biting her lip so hard I'm surprised she didn't draw blood. Fee had her arms around her brother who looked as if he was trying not to cry.

Dog sprang away from Dave, danced back a few steps and jumped clear of a weak jab. The Ross kids jeered. Dog turned, full circle, and as he came around he let out a roar. He dived at Dave, decking him with a thudding cross-punch. Dave fell back on the sand and Dog leapt on him, laid into him, pummelling him with both fists. I ran forward and so did Kit. We hauled him off. Ned and Ratty ran in to get Dave on his feet but he was out cold.

The Ross kids were stunned. No one said anything, no one called the winner of the last fight, no one called it best of five. I don't think they could get their heads around losing a contest when the odds had been so stacked in their favour. It didn't seem possible one skinny lad from Carrig Cove could beat five of the best from Ross.

I looked at Maeve. She glared at Ali as if it was his fault, pointedly looking at his untested hands. I was beginning to see how her mind worked. She'd deliberately put Ali last when she called the names of her challengers because she'd expected it to be over by the time it got to him. She'd probably reckoned that if it wasn't over by then, Dog would be exhausted and Ali would have no problem beating him. The one thing she hadn't reckoned on was Dog winning. She was raging.

Raging with everyone but me. She came over to me and kissed the cut on my chin. Ali saw and his anger slid into a curl of his lip. For a moment he and I stood there glowering at each other and then Maeve took his arm.

'Let's get out of here,' she said. 'Let them have their little victory.'

She turned and she and Ali led the Ross kids up off Ladies' Nook, Ned and Ratty dragging the half-conscious Dave Hannigan between them. I nodded to Kit and Dog and followed.

37
Emer

Blood was running down Dog's cheek from a cut below his right eye, his nose was pumping, there were bruises appearing on his arms and body. I felt sick to my stomach but stayed where I was with Fee and Rory. We didn't move, didn't speak as we watched the Ross kids leave the beach. Once they disappeared completely from view Dog crumpled and Kit caught him as he went down. I ran forward. I'd brought a thermos of ice from home. I tipped some cubes into my hanky then handed the thermos to Kit. He held it to Dog's mouth while I dabbed the cuts on his face. Dog let us tend him but kept his eyes closed.

'You were amazing, Dog,' Rory stammered, straining around me to see Dog's face. 'You beat them all on your own. Just you. You're a hero, you are.'

Dog attempted a smile; it turned into a wince.

'Did Gus McRoy win his fight fair and square?' Kit asked. 'I could have sworn you were getting the upper hand before he toppled you. You didn't go throwing it for old time's sake?'

Dog shook his head. 'Fair and square,' he said. He winced again as I pressed ice to his eye. 'How bad is it?' he said.

'You've been prettier,' a voice behind us said. 'And you will be again.'

We looked around. There was a man crossing the sand. He was dressed from head to foot in black leather, his eyes hidden behind large sunglasses.

'Hey, Seth,' he said. He took off the shades and I saw his eyes were two different colours: one green, one blue.

'Hey, Lou,' Dog said, squinting through rapidly swelling eyelids.

'Always something with you, eh?' the man said. He hunkered down and held out his hand. Dog grabbed it and they embraced. The man grinned and turned to us.

'I'm Seth's dad,' he said. 'Lou McCane.'

He turned back to Dog. 'The carnival is in Ballyfin for a few days,' he said. 'I had the day off – I was coming out to see you. Next thing I see a load of grim-faced kids spilling out onto the road in front of me, two or three looking the worse for wear. I had to pull over while they got themselves on their bicycles and away. I noticed there were a few bikes left behind so I came down to see if they'd left bodies on the beach or what.' He laughed. 'And here you are. What have you been fighting about this time?' His tone was mocking but I could see the affection in his eyes.

'He took on five of them, Mr McCane,' Rory said. 'Well, four. He didn't have to fight the fifth guy. And he did it by himself. It'll stop now, the messing. They have to stop it because they agreed. Dog won so we get to keep our dolphin and they have to stop coming to Carrig Cove at night and breaking things.'

Lou McCane raised his eyebrows. 'Sounds complicated,' he said. 'Seth can catch me up later. Right now I think maybe I should take him back with me to Ballyfin, clean him up, see to those cuts and bruises. Will you and Kit give me a hand to get him up to the road?' Rory leapt up immediately, clearly thrilled to be asked. Kit and me got up more slowly, easing Dog to his feet between us.

'You must be Emer,' Lou McCane said, smiling at me. 'Don't worry, Emer, I'll look after him and I'll send him back to you, good as new.'

I nodded and let go Dog's arm. Dog was in pain,

I know, but he'd barely looked at me since the Ross kids had left and now he only had eyes for his father. His dad was so like him, slight and wiry with the same eyes, same high cheekbones, same long dark-blond hair. I picked up Dog's T-shirt and denim jacket, Fee picked up the flask and we walked across the beach behind the men, Rory proudly propping up Dog's right arm, Kit taking most of the weight on his side. Lou McCane glanced at Kit's leg, taking in the limp. He stepped forward and scooped his own arm under Dog's.

'Let me, Kit. Myself and this fine fellow can manage, can't we?' he said, looking across at Rory. Ror nodded so hard his glasses bounced.

Lou McCane almost carried his son up the steep steps. There was a large black motorbike standing at the side of the road, one of those machines boys drool over. Fee looked at me and raised her eyebrows. Lou propped Dog against the seat of the bike.

'Could you help Seth get his T-shirt back on, Emer?' Lou said. 'And his jacket too. It'll be nippy enough on the bike once we're out on the road.'

He turned to Kit and Rory, spreading his arms wide as he walked, effectively moving them a few feet away. Fee went with them and I turned to Dog.

'Can you raise your arms?' I asked. I knew I had

tears in my eyes. I tried to swipe them with my sleeve as I held the T-shirt over Dog's head.

He grunted and lifted his arms slowly. I hid a grimace when I saw the state of his knuckles. I drew the T-shirt past his face and he saw me at last.

'Lovely Emer,' he said. 'My lovely Emer.' He leaned forwards and brushed his cut lips against mine.

'Tell his mother he's staying with me for a few days. No need for her to know the state he's in,' Lou was saying to Kit, Fee and Rory.

He shook hands with each of them in turn, then came back to the bike, lifted the helmet from the handlebars and placed it gently over his son's head. He helped Dog on, zipped his leather jacket up and climbed on himself.

'Goodbye, Emer,' he said. 'I hope I'll see you again sometime.' He held out his hand and I took it. Instead of shaking my hand he raised it to his lips and kissed the back of my fingers. 'You're good for him,' he said. 'I can tell.'

I stood away from the bike as Lou kicked it into life. Dog wrapped his arms around his dad's waist and leaned into his back. The bike lurched away, roaring up the road in the direction of Ross, Ballyfin and the rest of the world. Kit, Fee, Rory and me picked up our bicycles and turned back towards Carrig. I'd have to face Da's wrath for skipping out of the shop two hours early without asking. Well, Da's anger would just wash off me. I'd hold onto the look Dog gave me, the touch of his lips on mine, and his father's words, 'You're good for him. I can tell.'

38

Emer

After work the next day I met Fee and Rory and we walked over to the beach. Kit was already there, still limping a little.

'Almost back to normal,' he said.

'Why did Rinn attack you?' I said. 'What's changed?'

He shrugged, shook his head. We sat on the shore and tossed pebbles at the sea.

'Are you going in?' Rory said to me.

I shook my head.

'I am,' he said, already halfway through stripping down to his swimming trunks. He took a deep breath and set off into the waves with his bottom lip caught between his teeth.

'What's come over him?' Kit asked.

'Dog Cullen,' Fee said, rolling her eyes. 'All last night and today: Dog this, Dog that. I'd better go in after him in case he does something daft.' She stood up and peeled off the dress she was wearing. Kit wolf-whistled and she mock-cuffed his ear before running in to join Rory, who was still wading in the shallows.

'Stay clear of Rinn,' I called after her.

She waved back at me, caught up on Rory and coaxed him a little further into the sea.

'So. Dog's dad,' I said, turning to Kit. 'He seems nice.'

'Dog's the spit of him, isn't he?' Kit said. 'Lou was an acrobat with Fossett's for years – high-wire stuff. Now he's with the carnival that comes through Ballyfin every summer. He usually turns up at Deirdre's place for a night or two to see Dog, or Dog goes and stays with him.'

'Where?' I asked.

'Lou has a caravan.'

'Oh.'

'Don't be imagining a romantic Gypsy Rose job with painted flowers and a plough horse,' he said. 'It's a modern two-berth, complete with mod cons, according to Dog.'

'Still romantic,' I said.

'Lou is sound as a pound. He'll look after Dog. I

remember him turning up one time a couple of years ago. He'd come to watch Dog play his first match with the minors. Dog was scoring point after point so the other team worked a bit too hard to contain him. One of them gave him a right belt in the shins with the hurley. The coach wanted to call an ambulance but Lou said he'd sort him. Dog appeared back the next week, leg good as new.'

'I thought Deirdre was the healer,' I said.

'Dee's good with the herbs,' Kit said. 'She put some ointment on my thigh the other night. It stank like badger scat but it did the trick. Or maybe the poitín just distracted me.'

'She gave you poitín?'

'A little sip,' Kit said. 'Not enough to give me a head or anything. Speaking of heads, here come a right shower of them.'

I followed his gaze and rolled my eyes. *Conor and his crew. Great.* Kit stood up as they approached.

Conor nodded at us. 'We heard what happened yesterday,' he said. 'Did Dog really take Ross on by himself?'

'He'd no choice, had he?' Kit said. 'He didn't know you lot were indisposed, sleeping off Atlantic-sized hangovers. I'd done my leg in so I wasn't any use. It was down to Dog.'

Conor laughed. 'Done your leg in? Heard that one before. Some people will do anything to get out of a fight.' The lads behind Conor snickered.

I got to my feet. 'That's a good one coming from you,' I said.

All eyes turned to me. 'Rinn caught Kit a belt with his snout the other night. Kit's lucky his leg's not broken. I'd say that's a pretty good excuse for not fighting yesterday. You lot, on the other hand' – I ran my eyes from left to right and back to Conor – 'you lot are pathetic. You've done nothing but sneak around at night playing amateur guerillas.'

Conor flushed scarlet. 'We'd have been there if we could,' he said. 'There was something in that beer we drank—'

'Yeah,' I snapped. 'It's called alcohol, and if you can't hold it you shouldn't drink it.'

Kit swallowed a smirk. 'No matter, the day was won,' he said. 'It's been sorted without you. Rinn is ours – if we still want the fecker – and there'll be no more night visits from Ross.'

'Is that what they agreed?' Conor said. He glanced at the other lads.

'And no more night visits the other way either,' I said.

'*We* didn't agree to that,' Phelim said.

The others nodded.

'Dog gave his word,' I said. 'Are you lot going to make a liar of him?'

'Take it easy,' Conor said. 'You're right, we should have been there yesterday. It doesn't look good that we weren't. We can't have the Rossers thinking we left it all to Dog.'

'No,' I said. 'Bloody well no. You are not doing anything else, d'you hear me?' I was shouting now. Fee and Rory came out of the water to see what was going on. Kit didn't know where to look and I didn't care. It was over. This stupid dolphin war was over. The violence had to stop. What comes after black eyes and split lips? How bad could it get?

I took a step forward and practically stuck my finger up Conor McNessa's nose. 'It's over,' I shouted. 'Leave it alone.'

None of them said a word – they just stared. I snatched my sweatshirt off the sand and marched away. I didn't look back, but I knew I'd been shouting at the wind. It wasn't over. Conor McNessa wouldn't leave it. He was too proud and weak to let things lie.

39
Gus

'Who got one of these on their doorstep this morning?' Ali Matthews held up what looked like a mangled chicken foot.

'Me,' Ratty said.

'Me too,' Ned said.

'I got a pair of them,' Dave said.

All heads swivelled over to me. Ali and his mates were gathered in front of the hotel doorway, ten feet from where I was standing. I looked up from rolling a cigarette. 'Nope,' I said. 'I didn't get one.'

'I suppose that's because you beat their champ and the rest of us didn't,' Ali said. 'Are they saying we're chickens? At least we showed up and fought. They're the ones that bottled out, left it to yer man Dog to do it all.'

I shrugged. I lit the cigarette as if I couldn't care less and leaned back against the wall. What Ali and co didn't know was that Maeve was there, also leaning against the corner wall, but at right angles to me, out of sight.

'They've broken their own deal,' Ratty said. 'Dog Cullen said the fight on the beach would be the end of it.'

'We're not going to take this lying down, are we?' Ali said.

'No,' said Ned. 'I say we go over there right now and sort them out. Bring the fight to their poxy little village.'

'Would you listen to them?' Maeve whispered. Her head was so close to mine her hair was tickling my ear. 'Injured egos, talking drivel. What a waste of a beautiful day.'

'Gus,' Ali said, turning his head to look at me. 'Are you with us?'

I shook my head. 'This is not my argument, Ali,' I said.

'That's how it is, is it?' he said. 'If Maeve and the other girls aren't around to see you fight, Gussy-boy doesn't perform?'

Some of the lads sniggered. I shrugged. 'That must be it,' I said. Ali frowned and looked away.

'I want to see you perform now, Gussy-boy,' Maeve hissed, her fingers stroking the side of my hand.

'Ned's right. We'll go over there right now,' Ali said, raising his voice. 'No warning, no plan – just go.'

The other lads nodded and yeah-yeahed.

'Out in the open, in the light of day. Let's see who's chicken then.'

'Yeah! Yeah!'

'I've never made love in a cave,' Maeve said. She took my hand and tugged me around the corner. She kissed me, right there, against the wall, with Ali and the rest of them only footsteps away; them discussing war tactics and me with Maeve's tongue in my mouth.

'Come on,' she said, pulling away from me. She grabbed my hand and tugged me over to where our bikes lay. 'They'll be a few more minutes winding themselves up for the fight. If we go right now we'll stay ahead of them. By the time they pass Ladies' Nook we'll already be shagging.'

I glanced up at the bedroom windows above us – privacy, white sheets, doors with locks – but I knew the idea of flying along the cliff road with Ali close behind us was probably turning Maeve on as much as the idea of making love in a cave.

'You're crazy, Maeve Grogan,' I whispered, running my fingers through her hair. 'Dangerous crazy.'

'And don't you forget it,' she said.

Ali and the others were still talking tough as we got on our bikes and sneaked away, out of Ross, onto the cliff road, towards the little beach where Dog Cullen had single-handedly beaten the town of Ross into submission a few days before.

40
Emer

I'd had another row with Da. The drought had crop yields down and prices were soaring. Da saw a way to make a few more pennies by repricing old stock. I said it was dishonest and refused to do the relabelling, so now he was raging with me. When Fee came in to tell me what Conor and his lot had done last night I could see Da's lips tighten. I pulled her into the corner.

'Talk fast,' I said. 'I reckon we've thirty seconds before Da goes boom.'

'Chicken feet,' Fee said. 'That's what they did – left some on the doorsteps of the fellas who lost to Dog.'

I shook my head. 'Conor's a right arse,' I said. I waved at Rory who was sitting on the windowsill outside.

Fee laughed. ‘Conor must be an arse if he has you cursing,’ she said. ‘Never thought I’d hear Emer Monaghan using four-letter words.’

‘I curse,’ I said.

‘Feck doesn’t count,’ she said. ‘Speak of the devil, there he goes.’

Conor McNessa and the other lads passed the shop, striding up the street with their hands dug into their pockets.

‘His ears must be burning,’ Fee said, and she went over to the door. ‘There’s something going on. Will you look at the walk of them? Like they have sticks up their bums.’

I went over to join her. She was right. None of the lads were speaking, none of them were smiling. All eyes faced forward. A bunch of girls fell in behind them – Mary Ryan, Louise O’Toole, Karen Cox – whispering, and pointing towards the causeway. A group of boys were gathered there, Ross boys.

‘Come away from the door, Emer,’ Da growled. ‘And you can be leaving now, Fee Hennessy.’

‘Right you are, Mr M,’ Fee said. She pulled a face at the back of Da’s head as she went. I saw her stop outside to look around for Rory and shrug when she couldn’t see him. She waved back at me and ran after the group heading to the causeway.

I walked up the shop. Whatever those lads were up to, I decided that I wasn't going to watch. I'd had enough of boys and their ridiculous posturing. Dog was with his dad so I didn't need to worry about him. I didn't so much as look up from the stuff I was stacking when I heard the first shouts. It was the scream that made me turn. There was such fear in it. My hand halted in mid-air. A moment's silence, another scream.

I recognised the screamer.

Fee.

I tore off my shop coat, dropped it to the floor and ran out onto the road without looking either way. I ran to the causeway, towards the two groups of kids. They were at the water, frozen in strange positions, as if they were playing broken statues. Only one figure was moving – Fee, struggling with all her might to get to the water. Louise and Karen were on either side of her, hanging onto her arms. Fee was screaming, 'Rory, Rory, oh my god, Rory.'

Oh God. Rory must have fallen in. Rory was in the water.

It was as if I was running through wet cement. Everything slowed down and I couldn't seem to reach the causeway. I saw someone dive into the bay. Kit, disappearing into the blue.

Kit surfaced just as I got to Fee. He gulped in a

breath and went back under. I pushed Louise aside and took Fee into my arms.

'Ror was trying to stop them fighting,' Fee sobbed. 'He ran between them. He was hitting all around him, yelling at them, saying they mustn't fight, that Dog had said it was over. Next thing he was in the water. I c-couldn't stop it, it happened so f-fast.'

Someone ran and pulled the life buoy off its hook. A couple of lads came out of their trance, kicked off their shoes. They were about to jump in when Kit came back up with Rory in his arms. The buoy was tossed out. Kit caught it and the lads pulled them in to the wall.

Ror's head was lolling about like a ragdoll's and his eyes were closed. Arms reached down to lift him from the water. Someone got in beside Kit to help heave Rory upwards. Karen let go Fee's other arm and knelt down beside Rory as soon as he was laid out on the tarmac. Fee and me knelt down beside her. I kept my arms around Fee's shoulders.

'Let Karen work,' I said 'She's a first-aider – she knows what to do.'

Karen leaned her ear down to Rory's mouth and put her hand to his chest. A lad from Ross stepped forward.

'I'm in the St John Ambulance as well,' he said to

me and Fee, and he knelt down opposite Karen. She tilted Rory's head, pinched his nose with her fingers and placed her mouth over his. The boy from Ross began to pump Rory's chest.

'Oh my god,' Fee whispered, and she slumped into me with one hand clutching at her face. She was shaking. I looked up at the girls standing behind us.

'Mary,' I said. 'Go to the pub. Get Paudy to phone an ambulance.'

Mary looked at me, appalled. 'An ambulance?' she said.

'An ambulance, Mary. Quick as you can.'

She went running. There wasn't a sound from anyone as we watched Karen and the lad from Ross work on Rory, little Rory. He was so pale. He didn't move, didn't open his eyes.

Not then.

Not when his mam came.

Not when the ambulance arrived.

The ambulance men did everything slowly and gently, strapping him to the stretcher, hoisting the stretcher into the ambulance. One of them helped Fee's mam up the steps.

'What am I supposed to do?' Fee asked. 'Will they let me go with them?'

'Of course they will,' I said. I walked Fee over and

said, 'She's his sister,' to the nearest man. He reached down to help Fee in and I hugged her and stepped back. I took Kit's hand in mine as they closed the ambulance door.

Kit was shivering to pieces. There were tears running down his face. The Ross kids got on their bikes as soon as the ambulance moved off. The Carrig kids and the other people who had gathered to watch drifted away as it disappeared across the causeway.

'Come into the shop and I'll get you a towel,' I said to Kit.

He shook his head. 'I'd rather go home,' he said.

We turned back towards the village. Something glittered on the road. I leaned down to pick it up. Rory's glasses. Twisted and broken.

41
Gus

The cave was cool. We lay down just inside its mouth and stripped off, our bodies sweaty from the ride along the cliff road. Maeve's skin was glistening.

'The scene of your triumph,' she said, as she pulled me down onto the sand. 'You're the only Ross boy who won his fight. Come get your reward.'

If she'd known Dog threw our fight she might have understood why I instantly lost my 'enthusiasm'. I tried to explain it away by saying I was afraid someone would come down on the beach and see us.

'Let me on top then,' Maeve said. 'If someone comes, they'll get an eyeful of my behind and you can save your blushes.'

She spun me around onto my back and she looked down into my face, her hair a veil around me.

'Lie back and think of Ulster, Gus McRoy,' she said.

I let her take over, let her dictate the rhythm. I forgot about Dog, forgot about the fight, forgot about being seen. My only problem now was trying not to come too quickly, holding on until Maeve had had her fill of me. When her pleasure echoed around the cave walls I felt like a god, like Mick-feckin'-Jagger. Afterwards we swam and then stretched out to dry on the stones at the edge of the shore. I let out a long howl.

'You're bloody something, Maeve Grogan,' I said, reaching to pull her towards me for another kiss.

'Whisht!' she said, sitting up suddenly. 'What's that noise?' She looked up at the cliff behind us.

A siren, the mee-maw mee-maw of an ambulance. A red light flashed past the hedgerows, hurtling along the road heading towards Carrig Cove. We listened as it went around the cliff road and watched it drive onto the causeway, a child's toy rolling on a toy road. It stopped. When I screwed my eyes tight I could make out figures standing around, and a couple of cars.

'An accident,' I said, trying to draw Maeve back down beside me.

'Obviously,' she said. 'Someone is hurt. It could be Ali.' She stood up and began pulling her clothes back on. 'Or one of the other lads.'

'More likely an old-timer has heat stroke and collapsed into his stout,' I said, but I got to my feet and tugged my jeans up. We stood at the water's edge.

'There's Rinn.' Maeve pointed at the waves between us and the causeway.

I shielded my eyes with one hand and saw him – a fin, a tail, gone. Then a little further on – fin, tail, fin, tail.

'Are there—? There are!' Maeve said. 'Look, there's two of them.'

She was right. There was another dolphin in the water. The second one was as pale as Rinn was dark. One jumped, the other jumped, then both leapt together, side by side. It looked as if they were chasing each other, playing.

'Has the fish got itself a girlfriend?' Maeve said. 'Or just a pal?'

I put my arm around her waist and pulled her towards me. 'A girlfriend,' I said. 'Love is in the air.' I kissed her neck.

On the causeway the ambulance began to move, a slow three-point turn to face back towards Ballyfin. Its light was revolving and we heard its siren, but it continued to move slowly, creeping its way along the cliff road. I knew what that meant, though I didn't say it aloud. Whoever was inside had a neck or back injury, and the ambulance men didn't want to risk jolting them.

Jesus, I thought. *Someone's been badly hurt. Someone's in real trouble.*

The ambulance passed behind us on the road. As it went by there was an explosion of surf in the water. There was a chase, the dolphins were cutting through the waves, evading and twisting. There was no mistaking the raw aggression. After a few minutes we saw the fins go in opposite directions.

'Not love,' Maeve said. 'Aggro. That's what's in the air. That's what's been in the air all summer.' She shrugged off my arms. 'When is that brother of yours coming home?'

'Tomorrow,' I said.

'Good,' she said. 'I think we're going to need him.'

IV

42
Emer

Fee rang me from the hospital that evening. Rory was alive, alive but in a coma. He'd hit his head when he went into the water; it was possible there would be brain damage. They would only know how bad it was if Rory regained consciousness.

If.

One little word with the weight of the world spinning off it. Fee was hardly able to talk for crying. She and her parents were in the hospital, watching and waiting. *Rory is plugged into tubes and machines,* she said. *He looks so tiny in the hospital bed,* she said.

'Oh, Emer. If I hadn't gone in the shop to talk to you. If I'd brought him in with me. I should never have let him out of my sight.'

Next morning Carrig Cove was quiet. News of

the accident had leaked out and only one boatload of day trippers left the pier that morning. There wasn't a lot to do in the shop. I was dusting shelves when I heard the roar of an engine on the causeway. When I went to the window I recognised Lou McCane's big black Harley. That day on the beach seemed a long time ago now.

The rider stopped the bike at the end of the causeway and the pillion passenger got off. Dog, wearing a black leather jacket that looked like a cast-off of Lou's. He lifted the helmet off his head and handed it to his father. Even from this distance it was obvious they were father and son. They embraced and Lou raised his hand and waved to someone beyond Dog. I saw Deirdre Cullen standing on Main Street, waiting. She returned the wave but she didn't go to them. Lou put on the helmet, kicked up the stand, turned a slow semi-circle and rode away. Dog watched him leave, then walked into his mother's arms, and let her hug and kiss him. He looked towards the shop, to where I was standing behind the window.

Wait, I told myself. *Wait, like his mam did. Let him come to you.*

He left Deirdre's side and began to walk across the road. His hair was longer than I remembered. Despite the punishment his body had taken only three days ago, there was no trace of bruising on his face, no sign of stiffness in his movements as he came to me.

Let me be the one who tells him about Rory, I thought. *I'll tell him quietly. I'll explain how it happened and there'll be no more trouble.* I smiled at him and pressed my palms to the glass. *If I can make him see that this has to stop now, everything will be OK.*

If.

A little word with such a weight of hope hung around it.

Dog was walking towards me, he was almost with me. Out of the corner of my eye I saw someone else approaching.

Kit.

Kit's hand reaching out to Dog's shoulder, Kit's lips moving, saying words which made Dog stop dead. Dog's eyes were still fixed on mine but they stopped seeing me. Every muscle in his face tightened and Dog turned from me as if he'd forgotten I existed. He turned. He walked away.

43

Emer

I didn't see Dog or Kit again that morning. Without Fee to bring me bulletins I had no clue what was going on out there on the street, what sort of revenge was being planned to pay the Ross kids back for what happened to Rory. I needed to know. I needed to know because Dog would be right at the centre of it.

By lunchtime I couldn't stand the wondering any longer and I did something I hadn't done all summer – I went looking for Louise and Mary and the other girls. I found them hanging around at the phone box. Louise was working the water pump even though there was a notice stuck on it saying it had been turned off to conserve water. I was trying to figure out how to ask them what I wanted to know when they all began speaking at once.

'Oh my god, Emer,' Louise said. 'Isn't it awful?

'You don't think Rory will die, do you?' Mary said.

'You must feel so bad,' Karen said. 'They're your friends.'

'They're all of our friends,' Mary said.

'My parents have been grilling me about what happened but I said nothing,' Janet MacFadden said.

I kept my replies vague, let them pat and soothe me.

'God knows what'll happen Monday,' Louise said. 'You must be beside yourself worrying about Dog. I know I'm really, really scared for Conor.' She waved her hands in front of her face and I saw the Claddagh ring she always wore on her right hand was turned inwards.

'I'm worried about Dog,' Mary said. 'For all of the boys, but especially for Dog. He's so riled up. It's dreadful.'

If you're so worried, why do you all sound so damned excited? I wanted to say. *Why are you all aflutter, like brainless butterflies?* I bit back the words. They wouldn't get me the information I wanted. I decided to ask straight out, before they read the irritation on my face.

'Where will it happen?' I said. 'When?'

Mary looked at me, eyes wide. 'You don't know?' she said. 'Have you and Dog broken up?'

I shook my head. 'I've been in the shop the whole

day,' I said. 'Dog can't come in there. Da doesn't like him.'

'Oh.' She didn't hide her disappointment well.

'It's to be Monday,' Louise said. 'At Ladies' Nook, like the other fight. I must say, you could have told us about that. We'd have gone. To show our support.'

'It happened quickly,' I said. 'What time Monday?'

'Three o'clock,' Louise said. 'Conor and the other boys will be there for sure. It won't all be up to Dog this time.'

'Everyone will be there this time,' Mary said. 'We're meeting at two-fifteen to cycle over. You can come with us, if you like.'

I shook my head. 'I'll be working,' I said.

Eyes slid towards eyes and away again.

'I'd just walk out if I were you,' Mary said. 'I wouldn't let anything get in the way of my being there. Not if Dog was my boyfriend.'

'There he is now, with Kit,' Karen said.

I turned to look. Dog and Kit were walking towards Hill Street.

'I've got to go,' I said to the girls, and stepped off the path without waiting for an answer.

The whispers began before I was out of earshot.

'That was strange, don't you think that was strange?'

'He's not even looking over at her.'

'I bet they've broken up.'

I kept walking after Dog and Kit. I didn't try to call them or catch up on them, not with the others watching. I figured the boys would turn up Hill Street and I'd catch up with them then. They turned. I was still being watched, I knew, so I forced myself to stroll. By the time I turned the corner the two boys were way ahead of me, halfway up the hill. They'd broken into a jog. As I watched they went past Kit's house and past the turn-off to Dog's.

Where are they going? I thought.

They vanished around a bend in the road and I trudged after them. The sun was beating down on my shoulders and my sandals were sticking to the hot tarmac. As I drew closer to the bend I heard voices shouting, boys' voices, incoherent shouts of aggression and grunts of effort and the odd encouraging 'G'wan'. The racket was coming from Delaney's field. I looked for a place where the fuchsia hedge was thin and I could see without being seen.

Conor was there, JJ and Phelim and all of the others. They were stripped to the waist, doing jumping jacks and yelling. Dog and Kit crossed the field to join them, peeling off their T-shirts as they went. Dog called everyone to order. He raised his hands in front of his face and began to go through a series of movements, punching his arms this way and that, obviously showing them some proper boxing moves. They followed him, raggedly at first, then with more focus, till they were all moving in unison. It looked as if they were performing some sort of tribal dance. JJ O'Toole ran over to a heap of clothes and assorted bags near the ditch and produced a tape deck. He pressed a button and ran back to take his place in the group. 'The Boys are Back in Town' began pumping across the field.

It was too late. Too late to talk to Dog. Too late to stop this. These boys were going to fight. Dog was going to lead them. I was about to turn and leave when I saw Alan Murphy pointing at a hedge behind them. One by one the boys stopped jumping around and stared over at it. Their mouths dropped open and I followed their gaze to see what it was they were watching.

Red.

Red that wasn't fuchsia bells.

Red-that-wasn't-fuchsia-bells which rose and hovered eerily above the hedge like a red cloud.

It floated across the field, towards the open-mouthed boys. It took me a moment to realise it was insects, thousands of insects. The boys crouched as the swarm came level with them and one or two of them began to run as the insects floated down. Someone screamed but Dog started to laugh.

'They're ladybirds,' he shouted. He flung his arms out and raised his face upwards. Beside him Kit grabbed an insect in his hand and examined it.

'Jaysus,' he said. 'You're right. Frigging ladybirds.' He mimicked Dog and threw his arms out. Behind them the others frowned and picked at the insects landing on their skin to check for themselves.

'Ha, ha,' laughed Conor. 'They tickle.'

The boys held up their arms and faces and within seconds the swarm landed, covering shoulders, cheeks, foreheads, hands. Some of boys were more favoured than others. Dog was swathed in them, and Conor was too. Kit and Phelim got a fair covering. Only a few landed on JJ and Alan.

Philo's voice rang around the field, singing of those wild-eyed invincible boys. The lads began to dance around, shouting along with the tape, shaking their fists in the air and pulling faces. My stomach flipped over as I watched Dog screaming at the sky, his skin a crawling red mass. I turned away and vomited into the ditch. When I looked back I saw Phelim Roche jump suddenly and slap his arm.

'Fecker bit me!' he hollered. 'It hurt!' He began to swipe at the insects. 'Ow, ow, bloody ow.'

'Argh!' yelled Alan. 'One got me!'

Laughing and yelling and yipping, the boys swept the insects from their bodies onto the dead grass.

'What the fuck is this?' Conor shouted. 'What the actual fuck?' and they laughed and stamped at the sea of red on the ground.

'Come on,' Dog said. 'Let's get out of this field. We can go for a run up the hill and through the village.' He ran towards the gate and the others followed behind, automatically falling into twos as they came out onto the road. I stepped into the bushes, ignoring the brambles and nettles. Dog mustn't see me now. The boys ran away up the hill. When they'd gone out of sight I walked into the field. Thin Lizzy was still playing on the tape deck. Ladybirds were crawling about the ground, stumbling over the yellow grass. Others were lying on the parched ground waving their legs in the air. More were dead or dying, their tiny bodies crushed by the feet of the boys they had flown to. Three carrion crows landed near me. They began to pick their way through the sea of red. As I watched I noticed they avoided the living and favoured the dead.

44
Gus

Ferdia arrived home from his training camp on the evening bus. I had intended running the car into Ballyfin to pick him up at the bus station but I got a last-minute call from the hotel to come in and do an extra shift. I'd wanted to be the one who filled him in on all the insanity that had been going on between Ross and Carrig; instead he bumped into Maeve and Ali as soon as he got home, and they told him. I got back from work that night to find him totally fired up.

'What's it to do with you?' I asked, surprised by his vehemence. 'You haven't been here all summer. You're not involved.'

'If it involves Ross, it involves me,' he said.

'Don't get dragged into this, Ferd,' I said. 'This

lot just want you for your fighting skills. They know you're the only one has the beating of Dog Cullen.'

'You beat him,' Ferdia said. 'Maeve told me.'

'It was a lucky punch. He'd flattened two other lads before we fought,' I said, not willing to come clean, not even to Ferdia.

'But you think I can beat him?' he asked.

I looked at him sitting there in Dad's old armchair. He'd grown since he left in June; he was as tall as me now. His chest was straining his T-shirt and his arms were muscled and toned. He was pounding his hands against the arms of Da's chair as if he could barely contain his own energy.

'If anyone can beat Dog, it's you,' I said.

Ferdia flushed. '*He* doesn't think so. *He's* been saying he can beat me, that he's always had the beating of me and always will. He says he's the natural fighter and all the training I've done is nothing but fancy technique.' He made a fist with one hand and slammed it into his other palm.

'Who said he said that?' I asked, though I didn't need to. I knew already who.

'Maeve and Ali. They told me.'

'They're lying,' I said. 'They've never spoken to Dog Cullen in their entire lives. How would they know what he thinks, what he says?'

'They said he's boasting about how I won't have the balls to face him. They said all of Carrig Cove is saying it.' Ferdia was shouting now. His vanity was injured.

I cursed Maeve under my breath. She'd boxed clever, as always. I'd told her yesterday I was staying out of this fight and that I'd be making sure Ferdia did too. She'd acted as if she understood and then gone behind my back to entice Ferdia into her web.

'Maeve said you won't fight this time,' Ferdia said. 'She said you regret fighting last week and that you won't stand against Carrig Cove again because you're still a Carrig boy at heart. She said you've never really cared about Ross but that she knows I do. And I do.'

'Why?' I said. 'What the hell has Ross ever done for you?'

'What has Carrig Cove ever done for you?' Ferdia snarled. 'Don't you remember how they turned on us when we were kids? You were their leader, the one they all looked up to, but the minute they knew we were leaving they treated us like lepers. Jesus, I'll never forget that day. We were lucky to make it out alive.'

'That was Conor McNessa,' I said. 'That was all his doing.'

'And the rest of them are excused for being sheep? Is that it? You may be prepared to forgive and forget, but I'm not. They ran us out of there. Do you know how much shit I've taken from the likes of JJ O'Toole and Phelim Roche over the years? How many times they've gotten digs in about us running away like rabbits? Do what you want, Gus, but I'm fighting. It's as much my fight as anyone's.'

I'd never realised that Ferdia was so bothered by what happened that day in Delaney's field. I'd always seen it as something that happened to me, something Conor did to me.

'You know there's a kid from Carrig in hospital?' I said. 'He's twelve or thirteen. He may not make it, Ferdia. I don't know how he wound up in the water but it wasn't an accident. I'm not saying someone pushed him in on purpose, but he'd not be in that hospital bed if Ali and his lot hadn't gone over there yesterday.'

'Ali said the young lad went crazy and ran at them, that he was hitting and kicking and someone shoved him away and someone else sidestepped, and next thing they knew he was in the water,' Ferdia said. 'It was no one's fault.'

'Maybe that's true. But I still don't see what it has to do with you.'

'If I'd been here, this thing would never have gone this far in the first place,' Ferdia said. 'I'd have been on the beach last week. I'd have fought Dog and we'd both have beaten him. Then Ali would have finished it and Ross would have won and it all would have stopped there. Well, I'll settle this tomorrow. I'll show Dog Cullen who the real fighter is.'

There was nothing I could do or say. I gave up. Maeve had figured it perfectly. She knew once she got Ferdia, she'd have me too.

'Right, then,' I said to Ferdia. 'If we're going to fight on Monday you'd better teach me some of this fancy technique you've been learning in the Big Smoke.'

45

Emer

I went up Hill Street again on Sunday night. It was Deirdre I went to see – I knew there was no point trying to dissuade Dog from fighting. He and the other lads were on the beach, training. Deirdre brought me in, gave me a cup of tea. She didn't ask why I'd come and I wasn't entirely sure why I had. She asked about me, what I wanted to do after school was done. I told her about Da and how he wanted me to work in the shop. She said I should do what I wanted to do.

'Get on a bus,' she said. 'Leave. It's your life – go live it.'

She asked after Rory.

'He's still in a coma,' I said.

'What happened? Was it an accident?' she said.

'I didn't see,' I said. 'I was in the shop.'

I stayed less than an hour. On the way home I wished I'd told her what really happened to Rory, wished I'd told her about the fight planned for next day. She was the only adult in Carrig I could imagine telling. I nearly turned back, but I didn't. I'd be snitching, breaking the teenage code. I went home, went to bed and tossed and turned. I missed Fee, missed Dog, missed our night swims with Rinn. The summer had started so brilliantly. Now everything was wrong.

Please wake up, Rory, I thought. *Open your eyes. Live.*

Next morning there was no news from the hospital and Da was like the Antichrist because so few people were turning up for boat trips. There was a second dolphin in the bay now, a white one. Da thought that'd bring people flocking to Carrig Cove again, but on Sunday the white dolphin attacked Rinn in full view of the village. The two bulls went at it, ramming one another and biting each other's tails. The folk in the boats were scared witless. The last two trips of the day were cancelled and Da was forced to give people their money back. Dan put up a sign saying, 'NO BOAT TRIPS TILL FURTHER NOTICE.' By Monday the fishermen were pulling the temporary seating out of the trawlers.

I kept my head down that morning and stayed

as far away from Da as I could. I didn't want him noticing how preoccupied I was. He was spoiling for a fight – bit the nose off poor Mrs Kehoe for asking twice if we had fig rolls, snarled at Mrs Ryan for cribbing about the water rationing.

'Isn't it bad enough having to deal with it without listening to people whinging?' he said.

I'd made up my mind not to go to Ladies' Nook. I didn't agree with the fighting. I didn't want to see it. I was angry with Dog.

Why does he always turn to violence to fix things? I thought. *Why can't he see it never stops anything? I won't be with a boy who answers everything with his fists. I'll break it off with him tomorrow.*

I told myself that's what I'd do but I knew I wouldn't. It didn't matter what he did. I loved him. I loved Dog Cullen.

I could think of nothing else but what would happen later on at Ladies' Nook. I watched the hands on the clock turn eleven, midday, one-fifteen, two-fifteen.

Please make this stop, let them see sense. Please don't let anyone else get hurt. I was so engrossed in my thoughts I almost didn't hear the phone ringing out back.

'I'll get it,' I said, and ran to the kitchen, hoping it was Fee, praying it was good news.

'Hello?'

'This is the operator,' the voice said. 'I have a call for an Emer Monagahan from a Fedelma Hennessy at the Holy Trinity Hospital in Ballyfin.'

'This is Emer Monaghan,' I said.

'Putting you through now. Caller, place your coins in the coinbox.'

I heard a clunk.

'Fee?' I said. 'Is that you?'

'Yes, it's me,' she said. 'Oh Emer. Rory woke up this morning. He opened his eyes. He's all right, Emer. He's OK.'

'Everything's OK?' I said. 'He's talking? He can move everything? All his fingers and toes?'

'Everything.' She was laughing and crying at the same time.

'Thank God,' I said. 'Thank God.'

'I know,' Fee said. 'I prayed like mad. I promised God I'd go to mass again if only Ror would wake up, and now he has, so I guess I'll have to go.'

'I'll believe it when I see it,' I said, laughing and wiping my nose. 'Fee? I'm so thrilled and I'm dying to see you and Ror, but there's something I need to do. I've got to go. OK?'

'But I put in a whole 50p. We've still got fifteen minutes, at least—'

'It's really important. I'll explain when I see you, Fee. I've got to go. Give my love to Rory.'

I put down the phone, tore off my shop coat and ran out the back door. My bike was against the wall. I grabbed it, shoved it through the side gate and out onto the street. I leapt on, didn't even turn my head when a car blasted its horn at me as I shot across the road towards the causeway. It was nearly three o'clock. If I could get to Ladies' Nook on time, get there before they started fighting, I could tell them Rory was awake. I could make this craziness stop.

46
Gus

The Carrig kids were already on the beach when we got there. They started hooting and yelling as soon as they saw us, stamping the ground and making crude gestures as we came down the steps. Maeve had to forgo her flare for pageantry. We were all running at each other when she pulled the trigger on the little silver starting gun she'd brought with her.

I made straight for Conor McNessa. I'd spied him from the steps and I kept him in my sights as I ran into the chaos. I owed him one, had owed him since I was twelve. Phelim Roche and JJ tried to block me as I zoned in on their leader but I was determined. I shoved JJ aside easily but I had to hit Phelim a belt on the jaw to get past him. That left just Conor and me. At last.

When my fist connected with his nose it made a very satisfying crunching sound. His eyes went wide in shock, then squeezed shut in pain and he collapsed on the sand, clutching his face and squealing like a stuck pig. My hand hurt like hell. The bruises from last week had only just healed and the skin on my knuckles gave immediately, but it was worth the pain to watch Conor topple, to see blood spurting from his stupid wee nose.

The echoes from Maeve's starting gun were still ringing around the beach and I'd already done what I'd come to do. There wasn't another lad on the beach I wanted to deck, except maybe Ali Matthews, and I couldn't very well hit him. I stepped back and took stock of the madness around me.

Everywhere fellas were laying into each other, arms wildly swinging, punches landed, punches missed. A few lads were playing dirty, kicking and pulling hair. I grabbed Ratty McRoth's arm as he was about to rabbit punch a Carrig Cove lad who was thumping the hell out of Ned Cranny.

'Fight fair, arsehole,' I shouted into Ratty's ear before letting him back to it.

I looked for Ferdia. He was wading through a crowd of lads, dispatching anyone stupid enough to challenge him with ridiculous ease. He was scanning the crowd and I knew he was seeking out Dog Cullen just as I'd searched for Conor. I turned and there was Dog, right in front of me. I put my fists up automatically.

'You owe me, Gus,' Dog said.

I nodded and opened my hands, showing my palms in surrender. That was when I heard a voice screaming, screaming above the shouts and yells on the beach, screaming above the audience of cheering girls watching the battle from its edges. Emer was standing on the steps above us, her hands cupped to her mouth, trying to make herself heard above the din.

'It's your girl,' I said to Dog. 'What's she saying?'

He turned to look at her.

Emer waved frantically and cupped her hands to her mouth again. 'Rory's awake,' she yelled. 'He's awake. He's all right.' She came down another couple of steps. 'RORY'S AWAKE,' she shouted.

Heads turned. The lads around Dog and me stopped fighting. Fists fell, bodies slumped on the sand or struggled up to standing. I saw a Carrig lad reach down to help a Ross lad to his feet.

'Gus,' a voice behind me hissed. 'Gus, get out of my way.'

My kid brother Ferdia was a man on a mission. He had come to fight Dog Cullen and no one could stop him, not even me.

I tried to block him; he shoved me aside.

I grabbed his arm; he twisted me off.

Dog had his back turned. He was looking up at Emer. A smile spread across his face as he took in her words. Then Ferdia was on top of him, knocking him off his feet. A thunk as shoulder met chest, a thud as both of them crashed to the ground. Everything else had stopped, everyone had been still. Now bodies scrambled to get out of the way of the two grim-faced boys, rolling across the sand, locked in one another's arms.

47
Emer

For one brief moment the fighting stopped. Everyone looked up at me and I thought, *They've heard me, it's over.* Dog saw me, his eyes met mine, I saw a smile begin as he took in what I'd said: *Rory's awake.*

Our eyes were still locked when Gus McRoy's brother came out of nowhere and knocked Dog to the ground, going down on top of him. Dog twisted about. The two boys rolled across the beach, everyone scattering out of their way. Someone shouted, 'Come on Ferdia, give it to him, Ferdia,' and someone else yelled, 'Get him, Dog'. Then everyone was in a circle, yelling, and the boys on the ground broke apart and leapt to their feet.

I saw Dog's hand go to his face. I saw him

wipe blood from his mouth. He frowned, an angry puzzled frown.

'What the hell, Ferdia?' he said, spreading his hands wide on either side of his body. 'Why would old friends like you and me fight? This is about us and them, Carrig and Ross, not about you and me.'

'Are you too fucking chicken to fight me, Dog Cullen?' Ferdia said. 'You know I have the beating of you so you think you'd better talk me out of it, is that it?'

The watching crowd sucked in its breath, a sickening sound equal parts alarm and anticipation.

Please Dog, I thought, *turn away, walk away.*

'Come on, Ferdia,' Dog said. 'You're Carrig Cove, like me. I don't want to fight you.' He smiled, stepped towards Ferdia and offered him his right hand. 'And you don't want to fight me.'

Ferdia spat on the sand, almost hitting Dog's foot. 'I'm for Ross now,' he said. 'Enough bullshit. Fight me or admit you're too scared to take me on.'

The crowd sucked in another ragged breath. Dog said nothing. His face grew grim. He stepped back and raised his fists.

Ferdia and he circled one another once. Dog went in, quick and light, and sprang away again. He'd caught Ferdia hard on his chin. Another slow circling.

Dog hit Ferdia in the stomach. Ferdia got Dog in the ribs, on the ear. Dog folded slightly and his face squeezed up in pain. I couldn't bear it. I needed to look away.

I let the fighting boys become a blur at the corner of my eye. I looked out to sea. I saw Rinn and the new dolphin. The sea was a storm around them, as if they'd been turning and twisting in tight circles. Even from shore I could tell them apart – Rinn so dark and so familiar, the other dolphin practically white. At first I thought they were playing together, leaping together, but Rinn caught the pale dolphin with a thwack of his tail as they re-entered the water.

I dropped my gaze back to the beach. Ferdia was in control of the fight now; I could see that. He was laying into Dog, pushing him towards an outcrop of rocks.

'Look out, Dog,' I whispered. 'LOOK OUT, DOG,' I screamed.

Dog stepped backwards to avoid a punch and stumbled. He threw his arms out to catch his balance. Did Ferdia just take the opportunity to land a heavy punch or was he aware of exactly where that punch would send Dog? I don't know. One minute Dog was struggling for balance, the next Ferdia's fist hit his jaw and Dog was slamming onto the rocks, his body, his head, his back, smashing cruelly against that jagged unyielding surface.

He cried out. The beach went quiet.

Gus made to grab his brother but Ferdia threw him off. He raised his fists and danced on the spot, waiting to see what Dog would do. Maeve Grogan stepped forward and began to count, 'One, two, three . . .' The other Ross kids joined in . . . 'four, five, six . . .' Kit went to help Dog but Dog waved him away and peeled himself slowly off the rocks. He stood up. He flinched as he did it, but he stood up.

That look came over his face, the look from last week when he faced Dave Hannigan on this same beach, the look I saw when we were eight years old and Butcher Hegarty's Rottweiler was about to attack.

Dog's face, Dog's lovely face, contorted. He bared his teeth like a feral, rabid thing. His eyes went stone-hard. Every muscle in his body popped from his wiry frame. I saw Ferdia's eyes flare, saw his stance go from attack to defend, but he wasn't quick enough. Dog flew at him, fists flying, a blur of raw rage. The watchers began to cheer and jeer.

Ferdia tried to block the punches, holding his arms in front of his face to protect his head, but one of Dog's punches made contact with his temple and Ferdia's arms dropped. For a few seconds Dog was landing every punch and Ferdia's head turned with each blow, helpless as a punch bag.

Stop, Dog. Stop. Please, please, please, stop.

It was Kit who ran forward; he grabbed one flying arm and hung on. Conor McNessa grabbed the other. Together they hauled Dog off. Ferdia's knees buckled. He dropped to the sand. Gus McRoy ran forward and caught his brother as he fell. He collapsed onto the sand with Ferdia in his arms. Someone from Carrig began to count, 'One, two, three, four—'

Stopped.

Ferdia's eyes were open but his face was still.

'Ferdia?' Gus said. 'Ferd?' His face turned ashen. 'Ferdia? FERDIA!' His voice rose to a scream and echoed around the rocks. A horrified gasp rustled through the watchers. Hands flew to faces, hands reached out, hands grabbed other hands. People stepped back, shrinking away from the two prostrate figures. I felt my body swaying, my foot groped for the next step on the stairs.

No, no, no.

My eyes went to the sea. The white dolphin was attacking Rinn and even from here I could see he was wounded. There was blood in the water.

No, no, no.

I looked down at Dog. My Dog. I'll never forget

his face – the horror on his face as he saw what he'd done.

'Ferdia,' he said. He shook his head in disbelief. Kit and Conor let go of his arms.

He began to move towards Gus but he only took one step. He stopped. He frowned and stared down at his ribs as if he'd never seen them before. One hand moved to his chest, the other flew to his throat. He started to cough, an awful gurgling sound. He wiped a hand across his lips and stared at his fingers.

They were red.

He coughed again and blood spewed from his mouth, a terrible amount of blood. It covered his chest and splattered the sand at his feet. And then he was falling backwards towards the rocks again. Kit was trying to catch him – Kit was calling his name.

I couldn't breathe. Blood in the sea, blood on the sand. Gus weeping across his brother's body. Dog's face growing still below me, his eyes fixed wide, one green, one blue. Dog, my Dog, my beloved Dog.

I stumbled down the steps onto the beach.

V

48
Gus

The days between the fight and the funerals are a blur. Waking every morning to remember, *Ferdia is dead, my brother is dead.* Mam crying, crying, crying. Gardaí at the house asking questions, making me tell them what happened over and over again.

The funerals were unbearable. The hot weather broke the morning we buried Ferd. There was a thunderstorm. The sky roared. It lashed rain. My mam was dressed in black again, the black mantilla stuck to her face like a shadow hooked on her pain. She sobbed through the mass and held my hand so hard it turned white.

Father McDermott spoke about the awful waste of a young life, how gifted Ferdia was, how full of promise. He said Ferdia had gone to a better place. Ferdia would never grow old; he'd be forever young.

Bullshit, I thought. *This is bullshit. Ferdia'll never be anything but the lad who died in a brawl on the beach. He's dead. Ferdia's dead. He'll be forever dead.*

Mam clung to me as the coffin was lowered. She screamed as the first clods of earth were thrown in the grave. I'll never forget that scream.

Afterwards she made me swear I'd never leave her alone. I said hadn't I another year to go in school and sure where would I be going anyway? But I knew Mam didn't mean now, this year. When she said never, she meant never.

I saw Kit and Fee and Emer in the churchyard. Emer looked numb and Fee had her arms around her most of the time. Kit looked lost. Dee Cullen was there too, poor woman. She hugged me and tried to talk to Mam, but Mam turned her head away.

Dog's funeral was the next day. Mam begged me not to go but I did. I was the only one from Ross who went. All of Carrig Cove was there. There was a guard of honour from the GAA for the coffin. Lou McCane didn't go to the service – he didn't do religion of any creed – but he turned up at the cemetery to watch from outside the wall as they buried his son.

The Gardaí came around again – more questions. They questioned everyone, all of the kids who'd been there that day, but in the end it was ruled as a brawl that had gone wrong, a tragic misadventure. Ferdia had died of a brain injury. A rib had punctured Dog's lung when he'd hit those rocks. An artery had ruptured and he had drowned in his own blood. They had killed each other. There was no one else to blame.

No one else to blame.

Only every one of us. We're all to blame for what happened because we all went along.

Some days I blame it on Maeve – if she'd never tried to steal that damned dolphin. Other days I put it on Conor – if he'd just left well enough alone. If Rory Hennessy hadn't ended up in the water, if Emer had reached Ladies' Nook five minutes earlier, if Dog hadn't been such a frigging hero, if Ferdia hadn't cared so much what other people thought of him, if Ali Matthews wasn't such a smarmy shite – if, if, if.

But mostly I blame myself. There are days I catch sight of myself in a window or a mirror and for a split second I think it's Ferd. For a split second I hope. And then I remember his body growing cold in my arms on the beach and I can barely stand to be inside my own skin.

For the last few weeks of that summer the deaths were all there was – they were in everybody's eyes, on everybody's lips. And then one day I heard a woman laughing, saw kids racing their bikes along the street. Mam and me were grieving but the town had moved on.

I stayed around for a month trying to be there for Mam, but I knew she blamed me for not keeping Ferdia out of the fight. It felt like her grief would swallow me up, that I would disappear before I ever had a chance to be. I got out of bed one night, packed a few things in a bin bag, climbed in my car and drove away. Maeve and Ali were snogging under a lamppost as I passed down Tavern Street, his hand inside her blouse. Maeve opened her eyes when she heard the car. She didn't smile, just lifted the fingers of one hand in salute.

49
Emer

September. Back-to-school time. The rain was coming down. I waited at the bus stop with Kit and Fee. When the bus came I looked back over at the shop. Da was moving around near the till. Mam was upstairs in the bedroom window, her face close to the glass. She looked so sad but she tried to smile as she waved. I felt a sob stick in my throat as I sat down and the bus turned onto the causeway.

Carrig Cove was grey again, as grey as the sky above it. Dan and Jim were on board the *Ella Louise*, readying her for a fishing trip. Mrs Ryan was walking towards the butcher's. I saw Deirdre Cullen standing in the post office doorway, waiting for it to open. She had no umbrella. She clutched a long cardigan about her body. She looked wretched.

Fee was sitting beside me, her hand in mine. Kit was in the seat in front of us, twisted around to face us, his head leaning against the window. Conor McNessa and his gang were down the back, Louise O'Toole sitting on Conor's knee, shrieking. Mary Ryan was sitting beside Karen Cox. She caught my eye as Louise squealed.

'Some people,' she said to me. 'So inappropriate given the day that's in it. I mean, he should be here, Dog should. It's so awful. You must be devastated.' She shot another venomous look down the bus. I turned away and looked out the window at the bay.

The day after Dog's funeral, Rinn's body had washed up on Carrig Cove beach. It was torn and bloated. Dan and Jim towed it out to sea, far out beyond the bay so it wouldn't wash back in again. For the rest of August I stayed indoors. I stopped working in the shop and stayed in my room. I couldn't bear being watched, being stopped by Mary and the other girls, everyone asking me questions and peering into my face as if they cared deeply how I was, when all they wanted were more details for their very own local drama. At night I crept out my window to walk the beach and remember. I was relieved when September came and the summer of seventy-six was officially over.

The bus pulled into Ross to pick up the Ross kids. Maeve Grogan got on, holding hands with Ali Matthews. She nodded over to me, Fee and Kit. The rest of her lot got on behind her. Ned Cranny started to say something in his thick loud voice. Maeve shot him a look and he shut up. The bus went quiet. It stayed that way till we reached Ballyfin.

At the school gates Kit, Fee and me stayed in our seats and waited for everyone else to pile off before we got out. We stood around getting soaked, watching the other kids trickle through the gates. Then Fee turned to me.

'Are you OK?' she said.

'Yes,' I said. 'No. I'm terrified.'

She threw her arms around me. 'I'm going to miss you so much,' she said.

'I'll write,' I said. 'When it's safe to, I mean.'

She nodded and let me go. I moved into Kit's arms.

'Mind her for me,' I said.

'If she'll let me,' he said. We laughed, though there were tears running down our faces.

'D'you have enough money?' he said.

I nodded. 'Mam gave me a heap last night,' I said. 'I think she cleaned out the till. She said it was mine anyway, my summer wages. Da'll kill her.'

'Your da's a mean shite,' Fee said.

'I'd better go,' I said. 'The bus is at half nine.'

'The train to Dublin?'

'At two.'

'We'll be in maths then,' she said. 'We'll be thinking of you when old Horse Face is trying to force-feed us trigonometry. What time does the ferry get to Holyhead?'

'Around midnight. I'll be in London this time tomorrow.'

She hugged me tight. 'We'll be thinking of you all day,' she said. 'All day and all night.'

I nodded. 'I know you will. Give Ror a kiss from me when you get home.'

'I will.'

The bell for classes had done ringing but Kit and Fee stood and watched me up the street. When I got to the turn in the road I waved, then I was on my own.

At the terminal I kept my head down and went straight to the ladies' loo, picked a cubicle and locked myself inside. I leaned back against the door, closed my eyes and breathed, but only for a moment. My school rucksack was packed with clothes instead of schoolbooks. I peeled off my soaked uniform and pulled on a pair of jeans and a sweatshirt.

I was about to stuff my uniform into the bag when

I realised there was no point: I'd never wear it again. I considered folding it and leaving it on the chair so someone else could use it, but I knew I shouldn't leave such an obvious trail. I shoved it into the sanitary disposal bin.

It was Mam who said I had to leave. She said Da would go crazy, that he'd call Father Allan and I'd end up in a home for wayward girls.

'They won't let you keep the baby,' she said. 'They'll take it away from you, put it up for adoption. You don't have to keep it, love, but I want you to have the choice. I won't have some gang of nuns treating you like dirt. Because they do, the nuns in those places.

'You'll go to London,' Mam said. 'My friend Aideen will take you. She has two kids, but she'll keep you till the baby comes. There's enough money there to last a while, if you're careful with it.'

It was Mam who said to tell Fee to tell the school I got sick on the bus and that I'd gone back home. It was Mam said I mustn't phone or send any letters home, not till I turned eighteen and was no longer a minor. It was Mam who said to get out of my school uniform as soon as I could and to put some make-up on.

'It makes you look older,' she said. 'People will leave you alone if you look old enough to be alone.'

I took out my wee make-up bag and looked at myself in the mirror. My hands were shaking so much I dropped the mascara brush into the sink twice. I put on way more make-up than normal and when I was done the girl looking back at me was a stranger.

I fastened up the rucksack and touched my fingers to the pocket of my kangaroo jacket. The money Mam gave me was where I'd put it.

'Deep breath,' I told my reflection. 'Lots of girls do this – so can you.'

I hoisted the rucksack over one shoulder, opened the bathroom door and walked out into the station.

As the bus pulled out I struck a bargain with myself. One more time, I'd let myself remember. One more time and then I'd face forward, face the future, my future and the choice I had to make. As Ballyfin and Ross and Carrig Cove and everything I knew fell away behind me I'd let myself remember that night on the beach, the night right after the one when Dog and Kit had turned up drunk with Gus McRoy. That night when I was so sure it was all over between Dog and me that I went down to the beach to swim with Rinn on my own.

It's midnight and I'm wide awake. My body is used to this new rhythm and I'm longing for the cold of the water after a long hot dusty day. I'm still awake when my watch shows one. I roll to my feet, grab my towel and slip out into the yard.

When I get to the beach I look around to make sure I have the place to myself. The moon is bright; I don't have to wait for my eyes to adjust to the darkness. I shed my clothes and walk into the sea.

Rinn is there already, waiting. He whistles his usual greeting and then he's quiet, as he always is with me. We swim together and when I stop, he stops and lets me come close, close enough to touch him.

I know I shouldn't, know it's a daft thing to do. If he reacts badly, lashes out, I'm alone, there's no one to help me. But I reach out. For a heart-stopping moment I run my fingers gently over his nose, his face, and Rinn and me, we hold each other's eye. He makes a low buzzing sound, like a cat's rumbling purr. I feel it vibrate through my fingers and up my arm. Then he turns and is gone.

I wade back to the shore with that touch singing on my palm. A fierce joy surges through me. I feel as if I've spoken to the ocean itself and in response, it has called my name.

A figure steps out from the shadow of the rocks. Dog, my Dog, lovely Dog. His eyes – one green, one blue – look anxious.

'Emer,' he says, and he holds his hands out to me.

He starts to say how sorry he is about what happened the night before, but I touch a finger to his lips to hush him.

I smile at him; he smiles back at me. The dimples flash in his cheeks and I laugh.

I take his hands in mine and I walk into his arms.

Author's Note

The story behind this story:

This story is a re-imagining of the ancient Irish legend known as the Táin Bó Cuailnge – The Cattle Raid of Cooley. When Queen Medb of Connacht and her army march on Ulster to steal the magical brown bull of Cuailnge, seventeen-year old Cú Chulainn single-handedly defends the kingdom.

Dog Cullen is based on Ireland's greatest hero, Cú Chulainn (pronounced *Coo Cullen*) which translates as the Hound of Culainn. The original Emer (*Ee-mur*) was Cú Chulainn's wife. Maeve Grogan is based on the infamous and fabulous Queen Medb (pronounced *Maeve*) of Connacht, Gus is Fergus Mac Róich, former king of Ulster, Connor is Conchobar (*Cruh-hoor*) Mac Nessa, King of Ulster.

The Táin is part of the Ulster Cycle of Irish mythology. Most of the action in the original story took place in County Louth, which was then part of Ulster. This re-imagining is set in a fictitious bay in County Donegal.

https://www.librariesireland.ie/sites/default/files/media/file-uploads/2018-10/Tain-Bo-Cuailgne-doc-eng-2_0.pdf

I studied two translations of the story when writing this: *The Táin*, Thomas Kinsella, published by Oxford University Press, and *The Táin*, Ciaran Carson, published by Penguin Classics.

Ireland in 1976:

The island of Ireland is divided into four provinces and Ulster makes up the northern part. There are nine counties in Ulster. In modern Ireland six of those counties are in Northern Ireland – the section of the island that is part of the United Kingdom – and the other three, including Donegal, are in the Republic of Ireland (The South).

In the 1970s the sectarian violence of the Troubles was at its height and the border crossings between North and South were manned by the British army.

https://en.wikipedia.org/wiki/The_Troubles

Hurling:

The sport of hurling has been played in Ireland for at least 3000 years. It is played with a stick (a hurl or hurley) and ball called a sliotar (pronounced *shli-thur*). It is a thrilling game and is considered by many to be the fastest field sport on Earth. The GAA (Gaelic Athletic Association) is a volunteer sports association dedicated to Irish sport – hurling and Gaelic football.

https://www.youtube.com/watch?v=xcGZ8_1ua0I

Abú:

Abú (*ah-boo*) is a victory cry. 'Carrig Cove abú' translates as Carrig Cove forever or victory to Carrig Cove.

Sex in 1970s Ireland:

1970s Ireland was overwhelmingly Catholic. The sixties hadn't really swung in Ireland, change was creeping in very slowly. There was no divorce, sex outside marriage was frowned upon and contraception was illegal. Condoms would not become available to buy until 1980 and even then a doctor's prescription was required. This is why Kit goes across the border into Northern Ireland to buy a supply of 'johnnies'. Teenage girls who got pregnant were often sent away to Magdalene Laundries run by religious orders. There they were basically imprisoned, made to do backbreaking work and forced to give up their babies for adoption.

The Summer of '76:
That summer was one of the hottest and driest ever recorded in Ireland and in Britain. Tarmac melted, the reservoirs emptied, water was rationed. Even adults shed some of the layers of clothing which people were still expected to wear – vests, girdles, slips, nylon stockings, gloves. Everyone slept with only a sheet on the bed. There was an explosion of ladybirds (ladybugs). Yes, sometimes they bite.

Acknowledgements

Thanks to my agent Eunice McMullen, Michael Emberley and Bernardine Nic Giolla Phádraig, for all the valuable and honest feedback on various versions of this story as I worked my way through it. Thanks to my editor Annie Eaton, who loved it enough to take it on – it's been great to work with you again.

Thanks to John Ryan for sharing his hurling knowledge, to Tim Storey and Laurel Fiszer Storey for answering a hundred questions about trawlers and fishing, to Dr Michael Byrne for the quick check on things medical and to Marie, Bren, Danny, Helen and Michele for responding with such great memories to my Facebook query about night sailings to Holyhead. Thanks to Peter Walsh, Michael and Ber for checking over the information page.

I received a literature bursary from the Arts Council of Ireland while working on this manuscript.

The bursary was awarded to me at a critical time and enabled me to complete the final couple of drafts, the ones which got it over the line.